STANZAS
OF
THE DAWN

A Tales of The Horizon™ Book

STANZAS
OF
THE DAWN

From Records left in the Sea of Light
by the Ancient Teachers

With Commentaries by
L. Z. Dáin

TALES OF THE HORIZON™

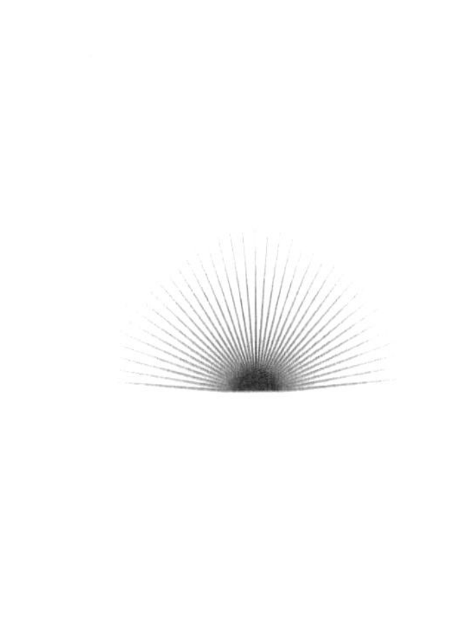

Contents

* * *

* * *

The Dawn

Dawn
of
the Age of the Magicians

Greetings! Seeker after Light,

Not unexpected has the Dawn of a New Day come to planet Earth, when the Human Soul will rise to heights longed for by poets, visionaries and their like. After all, the movements of the stars none can halt, and the Cosmic Clock in its march forward rolls.

Yet, the ending of the Night and the arrival of the Day have taken Humans by surprise. And their hearts and minds have to confusion, fears and even rage fallen prey. Nonetheless, everywhere on Earth today change is the order of the day.

The Earth herself longed for the Dawn of the New, and now that it has arrived she does her part — mirroring to Humans what their hearts must leave behind. Cold and heat, storms and droughts, fires and floods, quakes and the rising of the seas, are all born from Humans' hearts, and they show us what no longer we should carry inside us.

Here, in this space dedicated to the Dawn of an Age, you may find that which may light your mind and heart during these times of change and when the Old wants to fight to hold onto that which suffocates the Soul in all. No one and nothing can stop that which is already written on the stars, as much as no one and nothing can stop the Sun from rising in the east as day replaces night.

All what is here offered is a gift for you to take or leave. Nothing is expected, nothing is required. Yet, remember, Seeker after Light, you and I and all were made with wings to soar through the stars and further up, not to crawl through the caverns of the dark.

Welcome, then, and let's together soar high — the heavens and the stars eagerly wait for us.

~ L. Z Dáin

* * *

Stanzas

Stanza I

The Dawn

Before opening Her eyes, She knew *it* had arrived. Rising from the stone bench and facing East, Her eyes contemplated the rosy light of dawn coloring the clear sky. A wide smile crossed Her wise yet ageless face, and joy suffused Her whole being — the New Day had finally arrived!

"Time to start!" — She spoke aloud to Herself and to The Powers all around Her Who had with patient understanding kept the long vigil until Humans would once again awake to their true Self.

"The Age of the Magicians has come to Earth!" — Her mighty voice next sent the fiat on the four winds and far beyond the skies. Yet, there it did not end. Her commanding words reached high into Spirit's fiery sea and down into Matter's dark swirls. All were going to be marshaled for the task ahead!

With quick and firm steps She next descended the winding stairway from the Watch-Tower to the Chamber of the Voice while murmuring with contained glee, "So much to do! So much to tell! So much to unveil!" Midway down, though, a question arose in Her that halted Her descent: "But will they listen? — Most think awake they are, yet they slumber and dream in the belief awake they are."

Then, as an echo from another time, another question came to Her: "My name! Will they ask for it? After all, they love to entertain their minds and hearts with the minutiae of all things and beings, and overlook the Essence and the essences of the All and all."

'Harbinger of the Horizon' was Her present name; although once She had been addressed by another one — it had been so far back in time and upon another star that She had let go of those memories and remembered it not. With a shrug and a pensive frown She continued Her descent, pondering on what was coming next.

The Chamber of the Voice had been ready since the end of the Third Age of Earth — She had taken care of that. All She now needed was at its center Her place to take, attune Her mind to their minds, Her heart to their hearts, and speak Her telling to all who would then listen. The awake ones would follow it from the start; the sleeping ones would hear the clarion call it carried and, one by one, arouse to do their part. Yes! they were going to awake! Each and all were needed to create the New Earth and the New Stars so much spoken of by the Ancient Teachers in their wisdom and foresight.

That which is a mystery no longer shall be so, and that which has been veiled will now be revealed.

That which was withdrawn will emerge into the light, and all Humans shall see and together joyful they shall be.

That time will come when pain and desolation have wrought their beneficent work; when all dear things have been destroyed and Humans will seek that which they discarded in vain pursuit of that which was at hand and easy of attainment – possessed, it had proved to be an agency of suffering and death – yet Humans seek Life, not Death!

Remembering those prophetic words from 'The Old Commentary'* the Ancient Teachers left written in the Sea of Light, the Harbinger of the Horizon donned upon Her shoulders the Mantle of the Stars and went to stand at the center of the pentagram to do Her part in the new symphony of creation Humans were about to play and sing to make of Earth a star.

⋆ ⋆ ⋆

---

* *The Rays and the Initiations* : Alice A. Bailey : p 332 : Lucis Publishing Company, New York.

Some Notes to the Seeker after Light:

Multiple layers of symbolism are contained in the above Stanza — and in others that will follow this one. It is for the reader to find the one, or ones, their intuition reveals to them. There is not a right or a wrong interpretation of the symbolisms. It is all about Light reflecting through the many facets of the great diamond jewel that is Humanity.

A few commentaries will be included with the Stanzas, when appropriate, to set in motion the light of understanding. However, this journey is the reader's journey and not the Scribe's. Thus, disregard the commentaries when the intuition takes you along another path.

At times, in the Stanzas and in the commentaries, "the Harbinger of the Horizon" is addressed as 'She' or as 'He' since modern human languages lack a pronoun to refer to those exalted Beings who are impersonal and beyond all gender classification.

It is wise to avoid reducing the Stanzas and the Commentaries to a spiritual or a religious interpretation. Spirituality and religion are only two of many avenues through which the Perennial Wisdom has inspired and guided Humans on Earth since ancient times. Were the reader to do so, it would handicap his or her efforts to move forward and 'be more'.

Besides the fields of spirituality and religion, Those Who throughout the ages have embodied and taught the Perennial Wisdom, have also inspired and guided the development and the advances of the sciences, the arts and architecture, education, the art and science of government, philosophy, sociology, economics, and other fields of human expression.

With these points in mind, let's then start with the commentary for this Stanza I.

★

Commentary

The Harbinger of the Horizon is a mysterious and exalted Being, Deva or Angel in essence — 'mysterious' because She is as yet unknown to most Humans on Earth. Her identity is analogous to the identity of the Soul or timeless and non-spatial Self of each individual but, in Her case, for Humanity as a whole.

As Her name implies (and that one is not Her only name), this Being *does not* represent the ultimate goal for the individual human being on Earth. Her task is other: To guide and inspire all Humanity on its journey to a Horizon which will appear only when Humanity will have become One — The time for this becoming is now with us!

The 'Mantle of the Stars' tells us that this Devic Being hasn't descended alone from "the Watch-Tower" (i.e. the Realm of the Universal Stream of Mind~Soul). The Harbinger of the Horizon comes in the company of a good number of collectives of Beings from the stars, and from beyond the 'form' dimensions, Who are also journeying together with Earth's Humans and with the entire bio-sphere and soul-sphere of the planet. Together, They and we are now living and participating in the Dawn of the Age of the Magicians — with all the tremendous and wonderful changes which this Dawn brings for us, personally, collectively and as a civilization, and for the planet, the Sol System and the star systems associated with ours.

We are thus not alone on our journey, nor in the task ahead!

The Powers accompanying the Harbinger of the Horizon are also Beings of an exalted level in the great Chain of BEING that extends from the tiny beings whose essences *are* the atoms of physical substance to those glorious and inscrutable Beings Whose essences *are* the Universe itself, and all Those others who *are* the many levels of existence in between.

More specifically, 'The Powers' spoken of in these *"Stanzas of The Dawn"* are a group of several collectives of highly advanced Beings of Light, all associated with our Earth and Sol System. Some are Deva or Angel in Their essence, while Others belong to other various orders of Beings unknown to most Humans on Earth — for now. They include a collective of Those who once were Humans like us, mastered their limitations, became the embodiment of Love~Wisdom, and who today constitute the Spiritual Hierarchy of Light of our planet.

What is important for us while considering these Stanzas is that 'The Powers' guide, inspire, foster and assist in the evolutionary development of the Souls of the many collectives of beings who call the Sol System and our planet 'home'.

Seven Great Ages or *Consciousness-Cycles* constitute the entire journey of Humanity on planet Earth. Each of these Ages is analogous to a movement in a symphony — a symphony Earth Humanity is playing and singing to the stars. And in this symphony, the sounds of the ending of an Age play together for a while with those of the dawn of the nascent one.

The Fifth Age that we have been living has now reached its climax and is moving towards its conclusion, while the Sixth Age is dawning. Each of these Ages spans many thousands of years, and the Fifth Age will overlap for a long while with the beginning of the Sixth Age. Nonetheless, a new Humanity is being born right now — rather, *we* are being born as a new Humanity, like a phoenix rising from its own ashes — a Humanity who will gather the gains, and discard the limitations, obtained during its long journey of identity-discovery along all the previous Ages. Then, with an understanding and loving heart Humanity will offer those gains — and itself — to the many collectives of Beings who are the natural world of Earth, and to those in Sol and in the stars as well who journey with us.

The Age of the Magicians is one of the names of the Sixth Age, for indeed during this Age, Earth Humans will become masters of themselves, and in so doing they will be masters of the powers, faculties and qualities of their divine Selves.

The word 'magician' is derived from the word *magh* or *mah* in old Hindi, a word which came from the Sanskrit word *mâha* — meaning, *great* or *noble*. The title was given to the individual noble of heart and well versed in the Perennial Wisdom — *a wise one,* we would call that individual today. The word *magh* or *mah* was later taken and incorporated into their languages by Persian, Middle East and Mediterranean cultures, and its modern expression comes to us from the Greek word *magikē.*

It is unfortunate that Christianity, during the reign of Constantine The Great, confused the true Magicians or Wise Ones with conjurors and enchanters — of which there were a good number of them during his time and since the end of the Fourth Age, and which are those who use for self-serving purposes and for controlling others what knowledge they may have of arcane matters. Thus, during Constantine's reign the lack of discrimination and the ignorance of those who compiled the current Christian Bible, and the subsequent doctrine, gave the word 'magician' a negative and evil connotation, even though the Gospels speak of the Magi or Magicians or Wise Men who visited the baby Jesus at his birth — who were truly noble beings and had nothing to do with conjurors and enchanters.

The Sixth Age is destined to be the Age of the true Magicians or Wise Ones. The title of "magician", or its equivalent, will then be restituted to its original meaning and applied, once that Age is well established, to all Humans on Earth who will have mastered the higher faculties of Soul. They will be the guides and the inspiration for the creation of a noble and great civilization like no other planet Earth has housed — and which will reach out in fellowship to the many collectives of

Beings who call the Sol System and the stars 'home'.

'The Old Commentary' mentioned in this Stanza — also known in some works on the Wisdom as 'The Commentary' — together with other works, is a collection of "writings" from the earliest times of Humanity, in the Third Age and the start of the Fourth Age, left by its first Teachers and Guides. These Teachers were not Human but Devas or Angels of great wisdom who had come from beyond the planet to foster the development of mind, heart and form in the infant Humanity. They remained on Earth until the dawn of the Fourth Age, when they were replaced in Their task by advanced Humans from the stars, some, and from future Ages, others.

Those Ancient Deva Teachers, all along Their time on Earth, "wrote", "notated" and "depicted" in the Light of Akasha dynamic, live, multi-dimensional symbols of light and sound, series of them, explaining the nature of the One Reality and of the journey of identity-discovery for Humanity. They thus left a wellspring of revelation, with commentaries, from which the basic Teachings of the Perennial Wisdom have originated. After Them, all the subsequent Teachers of Humanity have drawn from those Teachings that which was appropriate for their times to enlighten the way of development of Soul in Humans and in all the collectives of beings who also share the planet with Humanity.

It truly can be said that all the 'scriptures' and so-called 'sacred writings' throughout history have been inspired by those timeless works left by the Ancient Teachers.

Those timeless, live and unalterable Teachings are thus *not* read in the way we read books. They are "seen", "heard", "touched" and "realized" — with the meaning being disclosed in a flash of understanding. To access them, certain developments in the brain and in the etheric, astral and mental bodies of the individual are required. Once the Age of the Magicians is firmly established, these Teachings will be commonly accessed by Humans, helping them to speed up their journey of identity-discovery.

✦

Thus, this Stanza reveals to us that the Dawn of a New Day is now with us… that the Age of Noble and Loving Magic has arrived, the Sixth Age… that we are called to awaken and to harken to the rising Sun! — and these are the subjects of the following Stanzas.

✦

Stanza II

The Triune Call

With His feet firmly planted inside the fiery pentagram of the Chamber of the Voice, and with His mind free from thought, the Harbinger of the Horizon let His gaze roam upon the panorama of the life Humans had created for themselves on Earth. Nothing was hidden to His sight — not even the Shadows' works, nor those of the Light.

It was thus that in no time He knew the first required task to usher the Dawn of the Age of the Magicians.

As He re-focused His mind while facing the East, the many stars in the Mantle of the Stars He wore shone brighter and clearer, flooding the Chamber with their unique and mighty lights. Blue, cold flames shot upwards, next, from the fiery pentagram, and power, renewed and mighty, surged in His mind as He prepared to make a triune Call.

Turning to the South, the First Call He sounded trumpeted throughout all the lands of Earth, forcing everyone to halt their doings and to harken to the Dawn:

> "Awake, mighty Ones! – Egoism... Insularity... Provincialism... mar your Light!"

Turning to the West, the Powers of Space carried the Second Call He sent along His breath:

> "Heart to heart and mind to mind – thus the many become One!"

Turning to the North, the Third Call, a mere whisper, was heard not only on this world but by many across the galaxies of stars adorning Earth's sky:

> "Space and Time are shadows on a wall – The One is All!"

✶ ✶ ✶

Commentary

Through symbolism, this Stanza tells us that three mighty *calls* or *summons to universality* the Age of Noble and Loving Magic is destined to hear:

> THE FIRST CALL is now sounding, at the Dawn of the Age, and what it carries no one can arrest or disregard. It summons everyone on Earth to reach out to each other in loving understanding and goodwill. It brings the thundering power to break down barriers, walls and all forms of separation

which delay the realization that, when all appearances are gone, the only reality left is the oneness of all Humans — each and all essential and unique expressions of The One Source of All.

The mighty trumpeting sounds of the First Call also dispel the illusion that made Humans think they weren't part of the collectives of beings who in their beingness and singing *are* the natural world of Earth.

One Humanity! One Planet Earth! — the First Call thus now sounds, heralding a wondrous Age and breaking down, in each, everything that shackles the free expression of the Soul.

THE SECOND CALL shall sound at a future time, asking Earth Humans to open their hearts and their skies to those from beyond the planet who are kith and kin. Then, a much-longed-for reunion will take place, dispelling the illusion of abandonment and loneliness haunting Earth Humans since the earliest times.

Yet, the Second Call awaits for the First Call to do its work — to awaken and to make of Earth Humans a One Humanity. Then and only then will Humanity be ready to sing in concert with the stars and the many collectives of those who travel together with us since the dawn of Time.

There is no date, nor a set time for the sounding of this Second Call. Only Earth Humans will in their hearts as One Humanity decide. But harken, reader of these lines — the Cosmic Clock moves of its own and waits for none!

One Universal Soul! One Community of Stars! — throughout the vastness of Space the Second Call thus shall summon many collectives of Souls to journey together, from then on, to fulfill their common destiny and be a Light onto even more stars.

The Third Call is the mightiest of the three. It will contain so much power that it will be carried in a whisper, summoning everyone on Earth, and many others from the stars, to master Time. It shall sound when the Universal Self who makes Space and Time will be recognized by each and all as the One Who resides in the heart. Then, Earth Humans and their kindred in the stars will discover the destiny for which the long and unusual path they have trodden has readied them.

One Life — nothing else is! — the Third Call so unveils the Mystery of mysteries to the many who shall then be One.

★

The First Call, which we are now living, is a mighty summons, dual in its effects — so are the two other Calls:

First, the Call enjoins everyone to let go of the limitations in their minds and hearts that veil the expression of their essential, non-spatial Self.

Each Call is an actual energy unlike those known to most today, and for many its impact is experienced as destruction, fear and confusion — *It does not have to be so*. 'Grasping and releasing' has been the journey of Earth Humans since its very beginning. Refusing to let go of that which no longer serves one's progress in the journey of identity-discovery along the Path of Return, or looking to the past as a refuge to evade changing, invokes into one's personal life fears, suffering and the forces of decay and destruction.

No one can ignore these Calls, nor shield oneself from them. The Age of Noble and Loving Humans is now with us, and it will continue relentlessly its appointed course — these Calls are not unlike the one sounded in the bio-sphere of Earth, many cycles ago, that brought to an end the age of the dinosaurs and ushered in a new and more noble age for the groups of souls of the animal kingdom then.

Second, the Call brings with it potencies and life-giving qualities that each and all Humans on Earth can benefit from. These potencies and life-giving qualities are an impulse to the New, particularly attuned to those who choose Love, Goodwill and Understanding in their in-teraction with each and all —including love, goodwill and understanding with themselves. These new poten-cies and qualities also make easier the process of 'letting go of the old' and of 'becoming more' — which is what the Dawn of the Age of the Magicians asks for.

Today many have their eyes only on the breaking down of that which has been dear to them, and they fear, con-demn and reject the rising of a more universal human-ity on Earth — free from any and all artificial divisions of history, culture, nationality, race, religious persua-sion, gender, and otherwise. Those who fear, condemn and reject are missing a great opportunity for personal and collective growth into fuller Humans, forgetting that all those divisions are not different from the clothes we wear one day and discard the next one after they have served their purpose.

To condemn and to reject others because they are different, think different, behave different, or look different, and to cling to separation, ignores the great and only commandment designed to guide the lives of Humans at the climaxing moment of the Fifth Age: *"Love The One Who sources All, and one another, as you love yourself."* When this commandment was uttered on this Earth by the Great Teacher, all the scriptures of the world were then reduced to ashes — nothing else was important. It is His injunction, solely and unqualified, that will carry into the Sixth Age those who choose to live by it.

*

The Calls to UNIVERSALITY *do not* intend to make of Earth's Humans, and of those from the stars, a homogeneous, standardized and uniform Humanity. Cultural and philosophical differences enrich Humanity and make of it a more potent whole — and not far into the future, Earth Humans will find out that their diversity is unique among the collectives of beings who dwell in the stars, and that it has made of them unique and valuable wise teachers and creators to many others. Humanity is truly a multi-faceted diamond jewel, which the evolutionary process is polishing to make it more beautiful and capable of reflecting to the stars, more powerfully and richer, the Light coming from on

High.

The Calls, instead of calling for a sameness, enjoin Humans to let go of condemnation, separativeness and self-serving attitudes… urge them to stop considering differences as something negative and undesirable, and to see them as a source of a greater power… and prompt them to cease ignoring that we — each of us — are truly our brother and sister's keeper and traveling companion on the Journey of Return.

The Calls referred to in this Stanza are so powerful that no one can arrest their intended effects, and that the birth of a civilization based on loving understanding, sharing, and a creativity directed to enhance each and all, including the natural world, is assured.

★

Stanza III

The Crisis

From Her place inside the pentagram of the Chamber of the Voice, the Harbinger of the Horizon felt the great turmoil that had seized Humans' hearts. Peace eluded them, made worse by the fears of the unknown and the fogs of confusion their minds could not dispel. Multitudes cried to the heavens and the stars to free them from the desolation that had descended upon all the lands of Earth.

The First Call has done its appointed task! — the Harbinger then knew. It had marshaled the awake ones. It had awoken others. And it had disturbed the dreaming of the slumbering ones, who, not knowing who they were, thrashed about in fear and confusion as that which was familiar slipped from their grasp.

The Spirit of the Earth and the many Essences of Nature felt likewise the Humans' agitation and sought to relieve that which was permitted by the beneficent Law, taken upon themselves some of what Humans felt. Yet, in their irritability and intolerance towards each other, and in their rejection of each other, Humans piled on the turbulences assailing them — making thus worse their agony. It did not help either their attempts to halt that which could not be halted — the coming of the New.

Heat and cold, gale and fires, droughts and floods, lava and quakes, disease and pestilence... had all come home to roost in loveless hearts.

"Their sorrows they created!" so The Powers accompanying the Harbinger of the Horizon said to Her. "Since the Fourth Age, cause and effect they ignore. The powers of their minds and their desires they bend to material ends. The seeds of pain and death thus they sow, forgetting egoism is the rot of mind and form, and that Nature mirrors them with the exactness of the Law... Yet, their journey they must travel to its end — there is no stopping nor retreat! Show them the Dawn has already broken, that the Love and Light it brings shall carry them through the dark hour to which they themselves have given birth."

The Harbinger of the Horizon pondered for a moment — yet not on Their pronouncement. She had for long traveled with The Powers and knew Their heart. Although Their words had sounded harsh, they voiced Their unending love for Humans and for the creatures of the Earth. No, Her mind was on those

She was about to summon so that They could be a prism to Her Light, and thus help Humans in their diversity through the crisis of Identity they did not yet realize it was their cry.

Next, rising above Space's many calls and closing Her eyes, the Harbinger of the Horizon directed Her inner gaze towards the flows of Time, to Those whose time was now a future one, and to Them She said:

> "Your lesser selves suffer and despair; in darkness they toil and fall prey to the unholy ones – Remember, You are them, they are You! Your loving presence shall light their hearts, lift their minds, and drive the unholy ones back to their lair – Come!"

Opening Her eyes and looking at the starry sky, She made another call, this time across Space:

> "Progenitors of Mind and Form! Your creations are ready for the Dawn of that Age in Your dreams You envisioned for them! – Come to infuse in them what You held and to unseal what You kept from them!"

And so it came to pass that none refused the Harbinger of the Horizon's call. In all the lands of Earth, contemporaries of the Age of Noble Magic were born ahead of their time — to comfort and to enlighten, to heal and to transform, and to show the way from 'now' to the 'then'. And also, all around Earth, many Holy Ones from the higher dimensions of the stars came to help awaken that which was still dormant in the minds and forms of those who in ages past had brought to Earth the seeds from Their stars.

* * *

Commentary

This *Stanza III* is a complex one, and in its symbolisms it addresses five related subjects: the inevitability of an inner crisis in each Human at the Dawn of the Age; the cause of that crisis; the response of Earth and the natural world to it; the inevitability of having to face the crisis and of moving forward; and the assistance of those collectives of Beings who are, in one way or another, intimately related to the Humanity of Earth.

Let's consider some of these symbolisms:

Similar to the other *"Stanzas of The Dawn"* included in this work, this *Stanza III* applies to each instance in which the Dawn of a new Age comes to Earth. It is, however, particularly relevant to the present time, when the psychological characteristics born in Humans during the climaxing Fifth Age are strongly colliding with those of the arriving Sixth Age, and when, for the first time in their long evolutionary journey, Humans feel inside themselves and experience this collision in its fullness. In the previous Dawns of an Age, Humans, in general, were less developed in mind and heart to be affected much by that collision. Not so this time, and the reaction of Humans to it complicates the present world-wide crisis.

As also the previous Stanzas indicate, this present crisis is not one of collapse or termination — much less so it is "a war of cultures" as some voices today shout from the rooftops. It is truly a crisis of opportunity and expansion for each and all, so that a more universal Human is born from it, ready to develop powers and higher faculties few remember they are natural to all, and ready to meet as equals those who dwell on the stars.

But the present crisis *is not* an external one. It is happening *within each of us* — the crisis isn't about cultures… it isn't about religions… it isn't about science… it isn't about religion versus science… it isn't about the inequalities of the economic system… it isn't about whether education is right or wrong… it isn't about the degradation of the natural environment… No, none of that! It is simply about the question: *Who am I?* — because the current crisis we all are living is truly a crisis of identity, in which the parameters that helped us define who we have been until now are questioned, and even invalidated, by new parameters which have arisen, apparently out of nowhere, in the hearts and minds of a good number of Humans who have decided they are done with the past and ready to 'be more'.

This *Stanza III* also throws light on the origin of the present crisis. It tells us that it is the result of the First Call the Harbinger of the Horizon sounded at the very start of the Dawn of the Sixth Age. This is a symbolic description of the arrival of a certain energy of a cosmic origin, coming from and through the core of our galaxy; energy which is directly responsible for awakening Earth Humans and all the creatures of the Earth (and, of course, many others in other star systems) to a new and higher level of BEING.

After the Fourth Age ended, we forgot about and became "blind and deaf" to the cycles of Time — to that grand interlocking system of cycles formed by the symphony of the spheres of Consciousness that constitutes Time and that rules Space. Yet, it is the observation of the great cycles of Time that will help us understand the reason that particular cosmic energy is now affecting our planet and star system.

It is thus that since the dawn of the Renaissance, our planet and our star system (together with many other star systems located in the same angular position as ours with respect to the core of our galaxy) are being stimulated by a certain energy whose purpose is to awake every being it touches to a new and higher level of existence and awareness. This type of stimulation sweeps cyclically through the galaxy at certain long intervals and lasts many thousands of centuries — this type of galactic stimulation accounts, for example, for the mass extinctions and the rapid appearance of new species that we observe happening in the history of our bio-sphere at certain long intervals.

Thus, there is nothing we can do to oppose the Dawn. Our only choice is to decide how much one benefits from it.

Yet this Stanza also tells us that our way of thinking, our desires, our emotions and feelings, and our actions, are all directly responsible for the way we enter the Dawn. It tells us that the present world-wide crisis is our doing, that it is our reaction to the arrival of the Dawn — but it is a reaction taking place inside each of us, which, when added collectively, accounts for the expression of that crisis in all the institutions of our civilization and in all the ways of living we have created.

Implied, thus, in the symbolism of the Stanza there is also the idea that the solution to the present crisis is in each of us — that each of us has to solve the crisis *within* by accepting and becoming the Love and Light the Dawn brings — which means, to let go of fears, rejection, intolerance, blaming, irritability and similar reactions, and replace them with love, goodwill and understanding for all, for each other, and towards oneself.

The fifth subject addressed, through symbolism, by this Stanza is not so easy to comprehend without the knowledge of the ancient history of Earth Humanity, specially regarding events during the Third Age — when the mind, the psychological framework and the body of the human being were given their present "structure".

Modern historians do not recognize those past Ages, primarily because no records, artifacts or fossils from those times are presently available to them. Nonetheless, records and artifacts from those times do exist and will be discovered by scientists in the times to come. Some will be unearthed as the Sixth Age advances. A good number of them are kept in the libraries and repositories of the Spiritual Hierarchy of Liberated Souls of our planet, and will also become available for study. Others will be accessed by those who can "read" the Light of Akasha. Thus, in future decades and centuries many will be able to access and study those records of the earliest times of Humans on Earth. So for now, this fifth subject of the Stanza is no more than a piece of information that most will not be able to confirm.

However, one important and indisputable observation we can all make right now regarding this fifth subject is that our Earth Humanity *is not* a uniform collective of beings, evolutionarily speaking, but that we are a collective of diverse evolutionary stages of development in mind, psychology and body. And this observation hints that the origin of our Humanity was also characterized by *diversity* — and to which this Stanza refers with 'the calls' of the Harbinger of the Horizon to Beings who are ahead in Time of most present-day Humans, and to those Collectives who dwell on the higher dimensions of stars associated with our Sol System.

Thus, both this Stanza and the Teachings of the Perennial Wisdom tell us that the origin of present-day Earth Humans cannot be explained solely as a direct evolutionary process from advanced primate forms, but that is also includes the intervention, at various points during the Third Age, of collectives of advanced Beings from dimensions beyond the physical, from Humanities whose development has taken place in other star systems, and from Deva or Angel Beings whose essences *are* Soul and Mind. Each of these Origins have contributed to our evolutionary development and to the characteristics of the mind, the psychology and the body of present-day Humans.

Diversity has, therefore, been a primary characteristic in the composition of our collective as Humans since our very beginning on this Earth — it has been and it will continue to be so. In this diversity is also hinted our destiny together with those among the stars.

A word of caution regarding this subject to the reader of these lines!

Time and again, during the long journey of identity-discovery that is our history on this Earth, some among those whose evolutionary development is somewhat ahead of others have used their station to subjugate, exploit, reject or condemn those of a less advanced stage on that journey. Even today we see this happening everywhere. This is a grave transgression of the evolutionary Law of our planet and star system, and those who have done that, or are doing that, have experienced and will experience the full application of the Law of Karma — i.e. the Law of Cause and Effect — in their own being.

To illustrate this point: At the end of the Fourth Age a crisis of tremendous proportions took place within Humanity when a number of those of a more advanced evolutionary stage twisted the-then civilization to their own selfish ends, and created a condition of extreme physical and psychological slavery and of exploitation of their fellow Humans and the natural world. Those Humans responsible for that transgression called upon themselves the full application of the Law and lost much of the evolutionary gains they had developed as Humans up to that moment, regressing to a condition that not even animal forms could house. Alas! Some of the acolytes of those individuals are with us today, seeking to follow on the footsteps of their former superiors by using the present crisis to their own advantage and with a thirst for power no matter the cost to Humanity and the bio-sphere.

There is, however, a higher natural evolutionary Law at play on our planet and star system, and this *Stanza III* also reminds us of it — *the Law of Love*. It tells us that the fastest, the surest and the easiest path to move along our journey of identity-discovery is by living according to the Principle of Love, a principle which was made clear to us by the Great Teacher in the words: *"Love The One Who sources All, and one another, as you love yourself."*

★

The Shadows and the Light

The Shadows, lurking in the unholy place, saw their opportunity in the ending of the Old and the Dawn of the New. To conquer and destroy, to deceive and to control, to instill despair, rage and fear, and to bring to an unholy end the destiny of Humans — those aims drive the quenchless thirst that from the start of Time has taken seat in them.

Alas! Earth, since the Fourth Age, a fertile ground for their plans became. Greed and separativeness, cruelty and hatred, lovelessness and insularity, and all the unholy faces of the ego — the Shadows feast on these and on those who to them give life.

Thus, from that which is beneath Space they surfaced to employ the powers of the Darkness to deceive and to control as servants the unwary ones.

And thus the times of tribulation took hold of those on Earth. Nation after nation, people after people in all the avenues of life became the puppets of their plans. The temples of religion, the fortresses of the wealthy, the halls of the governing, and the wilted hearts of the small-minded — in those places they found many who unknowingly enlisted in their army of deception and control.

"Free to choose between the Darkness and the Light, Humans are." So the Powers accompanying the Harbinger of the Horizon said to Him. "Just stand inside the pentagram and shine Your mighty Light far and wide. And in so doing, gather as many as You can to work like You and in the brightness of Your Light — make thus known, far and wide, that Love, Goodwill and Understanding are the shield to ward off the unholy ones. But Humans must decide, each, if to travel the Path of Light and Life they want, or the one which takes them through the dreary caverns of the Dark."

And it was thus that the Harbinger of the Horizon also gathered an army, but His was infused with supernal Light. Though an army, Love, Goodwill and Understanding were their weapons. To include and to relieve, to enlighten and to nourish, and to break down the walls of separation — those expressions of the heart His army uses to make of many a One.

✴ ✴ ✴

Commentary

The initial impression in those who study this Stanza may be one of hopelessness — after all, a great many Humans on Earth are still at the stage in their evolutionary development in which they are self-centered and may fall prey to the Shadows. Yet the key to understand this *Stanza IV* is in *the simplicity* with which The Powers accompanying the Harbinger of the Horizon respond to the war launched by the Shadows to stamp out the Soul of Earth Humanity — and in so doing, to thwart the destiny of the many collectives of beings who travel together with Earth Humans the Path of Return.

Thus, in truth this Stanza is one of Hope and Illumination. It tells us that shadows can never conquer light… that light, by its very essence, vanishes the insubstantial existence of shadows of any type. It is on this simple understanding of the nature of Light that Hope resides when today the Shadows seek to frighten us and thus reduce us to be their pawns.

This Stanza is also simple and direct in its instruction to those who choose the Path of Light — Love, Goodwill and Understanding are the tools, not only to ward off the Shadows, but to build a new civilization in which all Humans and the natural world can grow freely into the fullness of their potentials.

This Stanza is very appropriate for the present times when deception, confusion and fear-inducing words and actions are the weapons of those who want to divide Humans into multiple camps that reject and hate each other. And this observation leads us to ask the question:

Who is of the Light, and who is a puppet of the Shadows in the present world-wide crisis we are living?

Before we answer this question, it is important and necessary to acknowledge that in each of us there are psychological tendencies, thought patterns, and habits of speech and of action that resonate, some with the Light, others with the Shadows. It is for this reason that the main battleground between the Light and the Darkness is inside each of us — ignoring this fact and failing to take clear and decisive steps to end "the war within", makes of us easy targets for the Shadows.

Another point to keep in mind is that the only reason the above question should be asked, and answered, *is not* because it tells us who to judge and condemn, but because it allows each of us to identify the human sources of deception, separativeness and destruction in the present times so that we will not fall prey to them. The Shadows never show their faces directly to anyone — never have. They are masters at psychological manipulation and mind games, and always remain behind the scenes. All we can see is their work through those who have become their puppets.

And here is the answer to the above question — it is as simple as the response of The Powers:

"You shall know them by their fruits."

'Their fruits' — 'our fruits' — those of the Light, or those of the puppets of the Shadows — are:

The quality and the content of the words they

speak.

The actions they initiate and sponsor.

The understanding of others and the compassion, or their absence, in their words and actions.

Their respect, or lack of it, for the differences in others — differences of any type.

Their regard and respect, or lack of them, for the paths of all the many beings who in their togetherness constitute the natural world of Earth.

Their intentions to unite Humans so that, in their diversity and freedom to pursue their unique path, a richer community, society, nation and world shall journey together towards greater horizons — or the opposite: to divide and to isolate, claiming that alone "we" will be greater than others.

These and other similar considerations are the "fruits" that will allow us to know those who live the ways of the Light and those who have fallen prey to the Shadows.

Yet, a word of caution! Remember reader of these lines, no one who travels the Path of Light condemns others, ever, not even those who have fallen prey to the Shadows. Just let them travel their chosen path, while you travel yours in the company of those of like mind and heart — using Love, Goodwill and Understanding as the shield that fends off the Shadows' arrows, and as the tools to make of Earth a star.

As for the fate of those who have fallen prey to the Shadows, know they have added a heavy burden to their Souls. Yet, one by one, in a future time, they will unburden themselves and find again their way 'home'. And when they shall return, we will have our arms open to embrace them again as the brothers and sisters that they are!

★

The Breaking of the Morning

The night had pulled back, yet most still stumbled in the dark. So long had it been since they had seen Light, none of them remembered they had sight. It was a sad spectacle for Those whose vigil had sped up the arrival of the Dawn. The Morning had come like the first bumblebee in spring time, like a whisper during a deafening storm, like the twinkle of a lone star in a cloudy sky — few aware it was a loving and caressing touch of the Source of All, urging Humans to look up.

Battles had been raging nonstop — people fighting people, nation fighting nation, belief against belief, system against system, truth against truth, views fighting views — each seeking to impose its rule. Cycle after cycle, none remembered their count, zealous hearts had spewed their ill-feelings and venomous pronouncements to those of unlike heart, blind to Truth yet believing they were chosen and right. And so the darkness encircling the fighting ones darker it became as time went by, suffocating what was left of love in their wilting hearts and of reason in their ossified minds.

And it was thus that the rising Sun in the eastern sky did not come as a battle cry, nor sounding the drums of war. And thus the many for whom war was life missed the arrival of the Morning Star. It was the awake ones who felt, one by one, the new Life.

In — with each breath the awake ones took the Life and Light the New Sun brought to fill their hearts and minds, and in a trice they became Its very Life and Light. Thus, hand in hand, heart to heart, and mind with mind — they proceeded to build the life sought for in every Age by those of kind hearts.

"Be! – Shine!" the Harbinger of the Horizon enjoined the awake ones while pouring upon their ready hearts and minds inspiration, strength and that which made of them, each, a blazing star upon this Earth.

* * *

Commentary

The first impression this *Stanza V* gives us — in its outermost layer of symbolism — is that the Light of the New Day breaks forth at the Dawn of an Age when "the culture wars" are at their worst, when the cacophony of voices claiming they possess and *are* the sole "truth" deafens all reasoning, all kindness, and all respect for each other and for the natural and divine right to journey one's path in the freedom of the heart and the mind.

There is, however, another and more important layer of symbolism in this Stanza; one that is more practical, personal and less symbolic than one may think.

The Stanza tells us that at the Dawn of the Age the battle *within* each of us is very real and it becomes fiercer — the battle between those psychological traits one considers "good" and those one considers "bad", between one's "vices" and one's "virtues", between one's higher aspirations and one's duties, between the habits brought from the past and the freedoms of an envisioned future, and so on. But the Stanza doesn't stop there. It adds that this battle *within* distracts us from the opportunity the Morning brings, and that the best course of action is to face "the East" to receive the blessings of the rising Sun, and to breathe *in* its Life and Light — "the rising Sun" symbolizes our higher nature, the Soul or higher Self; it also symbolizes "The Powers" referred to in these Stanzas, as well as all others Sources of Light and Life guiding our journey. It likewise tells us that the incoming Life and Light will renew us in body, heart and mind and will ready us to receive the gifts the New Day brings — inspiration, creativity, the higher faculties of Soul, Initiation into the Mysteries, the path to offset Time and thus conquer Death, expanding relations at all levels of Space and dimensions of Time, and so on.

In a previous Stanza we saw that the so-called "culture wars" of the present times are more about "the war within" than any other thing. This *Stanza V* gives us an additional light on this subject — it tells us that those engaged in "the culture wars" are actually losing "the war within", and that their zeal and belligerence blind them to this realization and to the eventual futility of their militancy. They may obtain short-lived gains in the present but are actually losing the future.

This Stanza is thus more practical because it enjoins us to stop fighting "the war within" once we acknowledge it for what it is — and of course, any war without — and, instead, tells us to put into practice — and live by — those principles which our hearts cherish the most. This exhortation can thus be described as "the practice of replacement" — to cease giving attention to our frustrations with oneself and others, to our undesirable habits, to finding blame for our challenges and troubles, and so on, and instead give full attention, continuously, since morning till dusk, to that which is noble in our hearts, to that which makes us joyful and freer, to those thoughts and feelings that lift the burdens from our shoulders and make us feel good and upbeat, to that which makes of us truly loving to all... and so on. And as important, it enjoins us *to act* on that which our hearts cherish the most, because without decisive action no one becomes renewed and more.

Stanza V also gives us an important and relevant insight regarding the arrival of the Sixth Age worthy of commenting. It tells us that the New *is not* starting with a grand, planet-wide event, either catastrophic or beneficial, nor with an apocalyptic battle that will remove from the Earth the so-called "wicked ones". No, instead it says to us that the New Day starts quietly and unobtrusively, in the silence of our hearts and minds, in each one, and that, as the Age rolls forward, the accumulated transformation its energies bring will make of us the builders of that way of living that is a direct reflection of what is happening inside us.

> In the present times there are many voices claiming that a purge is necessary for Humanity to move forward into the New; or that natural upheavals are coming which will cleanse the Earth of "the wicked ones" and make life better for those who would survive; or that somehow those who have enslaved Humans through an unfair economic, political and social system are going to be "imprisoned, judged and made to pay for their crimes" — and so on the list of "prophesies", "conspiracies" and the like goes, each and all claiming they are right and even that they are 'inspired' from on high.

> Yet, the rising Sun of the New Day doesn't arrive with a big bang, least of all with the coming of a so-called "divine Being" sitting in judgment to split Humanity into 'the good ones' and 'the bad ones'. The fact is, the evolutionary process on this Earth hasn't finished with us; the Humanity of Earth still has a long way ahead to go on its journey of identity-discovery; the Sixth and Seventh Ages still have to play out and bring all their blessings

and opportunities for growth — these Ages will last many thousands of years, and every Soul incarnated today, as well as those out of incarnation, will cycle through them to arrive at their full potential as divine beings, expressions of The One Source of All.

Stanza V likewise tells us that the rising Sun makes Its presence known through Its warm, comforting, renewing and illuminating rays, shining upon each and everyone, with no exception, after a cold, dreary and dark night. And this is happening right now — the Sun of the Sixth Age is now rising in 'the eastern horizon' and is pouring Its beneficent rays to each and all, but it is each one's choice to take them *in*, or not, and thus become, or not, in this present cycle a star upon this Earth.

Many, many today in all the lands of the Earth are ready to take in the beneficial rays of the New Day. It is based on this fact that "The Powers" guiding us are certain that we are about to start building a new civilization — noble, kind and inclusive — and that, as the years and decades roll on, it will become evident to all that a new type of Human is emerging — Humans who are wise and noble in their hearts and minds, masters of themselves, creators of Space and of Time, and made in the likeness of Love, Beauty and Perfection. They will truly be the new Magicians of the Sixth Age. Nothing can stop this from happening.

*

The Dragons Rising

Warm and life-giving Its rays all those awake on Earth felt. Yet, deeper into Matter's dark swirls the rising Sun's rays also went. "Upright! Coiled dwellers of the Waters of Space. Rise!" — so Its rays commanded to the depths. "Starlight, your dark fire is destined to be!"

The Morning, this time, had arrived unlike those of yonder past. Though the din of battles still sounded near and afar, those awake knew a timeless magic in their hearts was rising with the breaking of the Morning. Awakening the seeds planted in the Second, the Sixth Age was about to bring forth the wonder of all time — the rising of the Dragons, the Masters of the Magic of the Heart.

And as night gave way to day, the noble alchemy of the New Day transformed all ways: Matter became Light, knowledge rose as wisdom, desire morphed into loving will, and the lowest and the highest met as one — Dragons of the heavens and the stars, love had thus made of Humans, and with them the dark swirls now reached to the fiery sea on high. The two Origins, Matter and Spirit, now formed a celestial bridge of Fiery Light made of those Humans who wielded the Magic of the Heart.

And so it came to be that, clad in Dragon Fire, those of Wisdom and Compassion had at last returned from their journey through the avenues of Time. The Earth now housed the Fire that made stars! — The Age of the Magicians no longer was a dream, though it was as yet a start.

"Be the Fire that warms all hearts! Be the Light that shines on their paths! – The sleeping ones, here and afar, cry for that." So the Harbinger of the Horizon prompted the Magicians of the Morning Star, whose love now bridged the caverns of the depths with the airy heights, making whole all by their very breath of sacred fire.

★ ★ ★

Some notes to the Seeker after Light:

> This Stanza VI is a good example of the language of Symbolism. In the Age now starting this language will become widely used for various reasons:

> First, the eternal Truths of the One Reality cannot be contained in any mental representation, less so in written or spoken words. Symbolism, on the other

hand, bridges the sub-conscious with the supra-conscious and, in so doing, 'speaks' to the innermost self in each of us, eliciting realization and understanding at the conscious level.

Second, the language of Symbolism cuts across cultural, educational and evolutionary-age barriers, and it is truly a universal language. These *"Stanzas of The Dawn"* are an example of this universality. They were used as teachings during the climaxing time of the Fourth Age and the Dawn of the Fifth Age. In those times they were phrased, not just in the human language of the day, but with concepts and references accessible to the understanding of the time. Nonetheless, as they so do it today, they provided illumination and guidance to those 'awake' at the Dawn then.

Third, the language of Symbolism is the language of those Orders of Beings we know as 'Devas' or 'Angels'. Everything in Space and Time that is a natural form or a natural process is a symbol of a deeper Reality, and both Space and Time are nothing more than the canvas on which the Orders of Angels or Devas express themselves. As Humans, on our journey of identity-discovery through Time and Space, we are thus immersed (until we finish our journey) in the creations of the Devas or Angels since it is their role in the grand symphony of the Universe to progressively reveal the One Reality *'as Space and Time'*. In the Sixth Age we are going to be exposed to dimensions of Space and Time that will portray revelations for which our mind alone will not be sufficient to reach understanding. Thus the importance of becoming used to the language of Symbolism.

With these points in mind, let's continue with the commentary for this Stanza.

★

Commentary

In spite of the high content of symbolism in *Stanza VI*, three ideas stand out from a first reading:

1. In the Sixth Age the energy of the rising Sun will transform not just Humans but Matter itself. This will be the result of a stimulation of the deepest and most fundamental of the energies of Matter — an energy which the Stanza refers to by the symbolic names of 'Matter's dark swirls', 'coiled dwellers of the Waters of Space', and 'Dragon Fire'; each of these names providing a symbolic perspective of the same energy.

2. The Magicians of the Sixth Age, those Humans who choose to benefit by its opportunities and blessings, will wield the highest magic of all — the Magic of the Heart.

3. It is through Humans themselves — through the awake ones, through those who take *in* the rays of the rising Sun — that 'the Dragon Fire' will reach out to the realm of Spirit, eliciting thus a transformation of the Earth itself, of all its Nature kingdoms and, of course, of Humanity.

Let's comment on each of these ideas in the order they

are listed here.

In spite of the great advances and discoveries modern Science has made regarding the nature of the physical atom, we haven't yet reached its more fundamental level. There, at that level, lies a type of highly charged energy circulating along minute, complex, self-standing patterns of spirals coiled upon themselves. There is an almost infinite number of these minute, self-contained energy patterns filling up the totality of Space; they exist at the most highly charged sub-atomic level, one not yet observable by the instruments of Science or the human senses in their current state of development. This vast "ocean" (i.e. "the Waters of Space" in the Stanza), made up of the most fundamental physical energy, constitutes truly what could be called *Primordial Matter*.

> These coiled, self-contained spirals of energy are the building blocks of the physical atom known to our Science and, therefore, the building blocks of all forms.

> Even though the term 'building block' is used here, these energy patterns *are not* 'particles'. In fact, in the near future Science will discover that there are not 'particles' at all inside the atom, that all the so-called 'particles' are nothing more than several types of energies circulating in unique standing patterns (unique according to their level), and that these patterns are held together by another type of energy whose characteristic is "cohesion". And at the most fundamental level — that is, the most energetic, the one with the highest speed of vibration

— are found the countless minute energy patterns of coiled spirals described above.

In our planet, the countless self-contained energy patterns that form this Primordial Matter have a number of their spirals in a condition of latency, non-radiatory, unlit, with just enough number of spirals active to produce the heat and vitality required by the physical forms used by the four kingdoms of Nature in their present state of evolutionary development. In this *Stanza VI* we are told, through symbolism, that in the Sixth Age this situation is going to change, that the spirals in latency will be awaken or activated, slowly and progressively, by the energies arriving to the planet from the center of our galaxy — this process will take centuries to allow forms in Nature to adapt to the higher energy content. We are also told that this activation will affect, most of all, the mineral and the human kingdoms. *Stanza VI* also adds that those Humans of noble and loving hearts will be the first to experience this "transfiguration" — i.e. the setting alight of 'the dark swirls' of Matter in the physical body.

In Eastern traditions knowledge of this activation of 'the fire of Matter' has been preserved in the teachings on "the kundalini fire". However, a lot of imaginative, spurious thinking and superstition surround these teachings, and only the general outline should be taken as instructive. The main point is — and *Stanza VI* makes it clear — this is a natural process on the path of awakening to one's higher nature, that it shouldn't be forced, and that the fundamental requirement for its rising, and as protection for the body, is for one to become Love itself — that is, to be the embodiment of the energy and consciousness of the Soul. This Soul energy, once it permeates the physical form (and it has to happen in a factual way, not in an aspirational way), it readies it for the activation of the latent spirals coiled in the atoms that form the physical body. Since this is a natural process, it also follows a precise pattern of activation and 'rising' in the body along the spinal column, setting the body ablaze with a cold fiery light. This subject is, however, long and complex, and is beyond this commentary.

Nonetheless, the main idea regarding this subject, and which *Stanza VI* tells us about, is that this 'rising of the Dragon Fire' in our forms is *an effect* of the transformation in consciousness — in our mind, in our psychological nature, and in our way of living — which the Path of Return entails. This transformation in consciousness is being accelerated, now, by the rising Sun of the New Day, and each of us can either work with it or take the slow and trying path.

Regarding the second idea presented in *Stanza VI* through symbolism — the Magic of the Heart — the Stanza could just have used the term "Magic" alone and unqualified, instead of using the expression, "the Magic of the Heart". There is, however, a powerful reason for this qualification.

Magic is an art and a science that has generated a lot of attention since the end of the Fourth Age. For some individuals of unselfish mind, it has been the subject of serious studies; for others, it has been the pursuit of power for self-serving purposes; and still for others, it has been the target of derision, rejection or condemnation. Yet in fact, very few truly have understood, and understand, what Magic is.

It would take us too long to consider here all those many misconceptions of Magic throughout history and in the present time. Sufficient is to say that all those misconceptions — from the attempts of primitive peoples to beg Nature for its blessings, to the efforts of conjurers and enchanters to exploit forces of which they have little or no knowledge, to the current entertainment industry dedicated to a spurious view of Magic and of super-powers that have nothing to do with the real thing — all of them are echoes in the subconscious of most Humans of the real nature of the Soul or Self in each of us.

Understanding Magic comes down to a simple fact regarding us, Humans:

Each of us is a Creator, endowed with the power to be a master of Space and Time and to free oneself from the limitations imposed by both.

But our essential nature doesn't end there. We are also Love itself — we are both the Love of God and the God of Love in manifestation; we are, in this Universe, the direct expression, extension and embodiment (all these terms are valid) of the Love aspect of The One Source of All. Still more, we are also that Will that sacrifices itself for the good of all — it is this Will that prompted us, Humans, to clothe ourselves in Time and Space, to blind ourselves to our true Identity and then start a journey of identity-discovery to show the way back to the Most High to many other Orders of Beings.

Thus, it is our essence to be Creators — Masters of Space and Time — yet Creators motivated by Love and willing to sacrifice ourselves to show others that they, similar to us, *are* The One Source of All in manifestation, and that The One Source of All is indeed Love.

When this *Stanza VI* speaks of "the Magic of the Heart", it refers to that — to our essential nature as Creators whose awareness is all-inclusive and whose power is used for the greatest good of all.

During the Sixth Age a large number of Humans on our Earth will reach the stage on the journey of identity-discovery where they will remember that they *are* "the Magic of the Heart". This will be a progressive event, which has already started, and which will be responsible for the creation of a civilization that will truly reflect "the Heart" or essential Human nature.

The third subject expressed in this *Stanza VI* — the rising of the Dragon Fire to the realm of Spirit and the subsequent transformation of the Earth — is the natural result of the two events commented on the previous two subjects.

The rising Sun announcing the Morning of the Sixth Age — i.e. the entrance of our Sol System and planet into that area of our galaxy where there is a powerful energy of transformation at the most essential level —

is responsible for awakening both, 'Matter's dark swirls' in the planet and the essence of Humans in their forms (i.e. the Soul essence *in* the persona and body). It is the combined work of these two awakenings that will elicit a transformation of the planet at various levels. The reason both these essences can work together is because they are harmonics of each other; that is, they are the same essential Fire — one active, awake and endowed with self-consciousness (the Human Soul), the other still dormant, waiting to be awakened to play its role (Matter's dark swirls).

This whole idea is expressed in *Stanza VI* with the phase, *"Awakening the seeds planted in the Second, the Sixth Age was about to bring forth the wonders of all time."* The meaning of this verse is that during the Second Age 'the Dragon Fire that is the Human Soul' made direct contact with 'the dark swirls' of Matter that were then forming our physical planet, and a close relationship was established between the two. This process was all part of the Plan that gave birth to and guides the evolutionary development of our Sol System and planet.

What is this Plan? — It is during the Sixth Age that we are going be ready, mentally and psychologically, and having the needed physical refinement, to find the answer to this question. Then wonder and joy will fill our hearts because we, ourselves, came up with that Plan, whose blessings will reach out far away to expanses beyond our galaxy.

As for the use of the word *'dragon'* in these Stanzas, and by many teachings on the Perennial Wisdom, this is a mystery whose origin lies in the group of stars called

Draco — a constellation stretching around the north celestial pole. The Perennial Wisdom teaches that there is a close relationship between stars in that constellation and our Sun and our Earth. That from that constellation came to our Sol System, and particularly to our planet, that energy which infused Matter with Mind-Soul — i.e. the building energy of the Universe.

The word 'dragon' in our modern European languages comes from the Greek word *drakōn* — meaning, *serpent.* The word for it in Sanskrit is *naga* — also meaning, *serpent.* Both words have been used widely in the Perennial Wisdom since times immemorial, for symbolic purposes. Important to notice in the symbolism is that serpents slither upon the ground, being pinned by gravity to it, while dragons have the freedom of the air, the sky and the heavens, unconstrained by the forces of Space.

Whether dragons existed in olden times on Earth as a distinct species of animals, is a matter for researchers to settle. It is to notice, however, that in Eastern traditions and folklore dragons are not considered to be some sort of animal, as they are in Western folklore. In the East they are regarded as an allegory of some Orders of Devas or Angels associated with the Law of Attraction, and its subsidiary natural laws — Devas whose essence expresses in Time and Space as a spiraling, or serpent-like, flowing energy; suggesting that the analogy to serpents may have appeared because of the sinuous displacement of their bodies, spiral-like. Thus, the true 'dragons' are those Orders of Devas.

*

Even though this *Stanza VI* deals with subjects that affect us and the planet directly, it is still a complex one whose ideas, for the most part, we aren't yet able to confirm by ourselves. Nonetheless, the Stanza ends with a practical injunction for all of us in the words of the Harbinger of the Horizon:

"Be the Fire that warms all hearts! Be the Light that shines on their paths! — The sleeping ones, here and afar, cry for that."

This injunction is both about the Love and Light that one can be *right now,* and about that greater Love and Light that we will become as the New Day advances, because in the end that is what each of us was, is and will forever be — Love, Creative Light, and the Will that chooses to use these to assist those who are still asleep to the realization that not only The One Source of All is in everyone, but that we all are the One Source Itself.

★

Stanza VII

The Temple of the Mysteries

Clear from smoke and foul clouds the sky became, and so did many hearts and minds. Exhausted of conflict, war and pain, Humans had laid down their arms. Nothing had been gained with their age-long crusades. Yet, free from the ancient curse now they were. A sacred emptiness was all that was left, and a sigh of relief from the Earth was heard.

In silence Humans and Angels awaited, in the company of the creatures of land, sea, air and fire, while the Morning the rising Sun slowly warmed up. What was impending none knew, though some whispered they heard an ancient echo resounding in the emptiness — a promise made to all at the start of their journey through Space and Time.

A Silence had likewise descended upon the Watch-Tower. Yet unlike the silent emptiness in human minds and hearts, pregnant with Life and Power the Silence in the Tower was. For eons The Powers and the Harbinger of the Horizon had readied themselves to sing the Song about to start. And so had the heavens and the stars.

Its first harmonies caught most unaware. Such a majestic Song Humans and Angels had never heard, and wonder rose in them. But that was not all. Upon hearing the mighty harmonies, like a dancer who has lost her step, the Earth herself stumbled from here to there — the Song was also new to her; besides, her guiding star no longer was there. Sol though came to her aid, and lovingly sent a fiery breath. Cold and transforming it was felt. A shift came next, and — Humans, Angels, Nature and Earth — all re-dressed themselves. The rays of a new guiding star had made their new dress while The Powers and the Harbinger together sang:

> The Temple has been remade!
> That which had been veiled,
> eyes will see it once again.
> That which was withdrawn,
> the light of day it will bring forth again.
> No longer shall the Mysteries be a mystery,
> And in the Light from on High
> Humans will walk once again.

Harken! – The twain is no more!

Rejoice, Humans and Angels! – Join in the Song!

* * *

Commentary

This *Stanza VII* is one of the most beautiful of the *"Stanzas of The Dawn"*. It speaks of the transformation which the Sixth Age will bring to Humans, to Devas or Angels, to the natural world, and to the Earth herself — once "the ancient curse" afflicting Humans will be exhausted. It also contains some verses regarding changes in the forms of Humans and Devas, and in the planet itself, changes which could be interpreted as prophetic and which speak of a re-making of "the Temple of the Mysteries".

Let's comment on each of these points.

The two expressions in this Stanza — *"free from the ancient curse"* and *"The twain is no more"* — refer to the same event; an event in consciousness that took place in Humans at the climaxing time of the Third Age and the dawn of the Fourth Age. It was this event that gave origin to Religion, as we know it today, and to the many ills of the civilizations since then, including the ills of our current civilization — materialism, inequality, poverty, crime, racism, oppression, separatism, proselytism, warmongering, militarism, damage to the environment, etc. — the list could go on, but the point is that all these ills spring from one and only one event that took place in the human consciousness in that far past.

As previous Stanzas have told us, from their very beginning Humans on this Earth have been characterized by *diversity* — a spiritual, mental, psychological and phenotypical diversity — and have held diverse evolutionary developments, forming a stairway of states of consciousness that spans from the less evolved to the most advanced ones. At the time here referred, there were three main groups of Humans on Earth, each forming their own civilization and each, of course, with certain degrees of diversity within them.

One group was integrated by those Humans whose origin was from this Earth and who had evolved, phenotypically, from a few advanced hominid species of the animal kingdom at the very start of the Third Age — species which then became extinct and of which nothing is known today by Archeology and Anthropology, but whose fossils and the imprints they left the Sixth Age will reveal.

Strictly speaking, those Humans didn't have an integrated and true civilization like the other two groups, but were about three dozen types of primitive Humans, spread throughout most of the lands of the planet, and each living clustered together in clans or tribes, with each of them no larger than a few thousand individuals. Some had a small degree of interchange with other groups, but not that much. Some were in a simple agrarian state of development, others were nomads, and still others were too primitive and lived in an almost-animal condition.

This first main group of Humans were physically- and instinctively-oriented in their awareness, had coarse bodies of various types, possessed a small recognition of desire, but not mental development — yet they were intelligent to a degree.

A second group was integrated by Humans who had started their evolutionary journey somewhere else in our solar system, and who had come to Earth when events on their native planets had forced their relocation. Originally they were of two main types; however, as time went by, Human Souls/Selves also from other spheres in the solar system started incarnating among them. They all eventually formed together their own civilization on one of the continental lands of the planet; a civilization characterized by a militant and entrepreneurial way of living.

This second main group of Humans were desire-driven individuals, emotionally polarized, possessed an incipient intellect and a mind beginning to be creative, and had a physical form somewhat athletic but not refined or graceful.

A third group was integrated by Humans who were much more advanced in their evolution than the second group, and whose origin was from other star systems. They came to Earth attracted by the unusual lushness and beauty of its bio-sphere and soul-sphere, by the evolutionary and psychological diversity of its Humans, and by the mysterious harmonies in the planet's Song broadcast far and beyond. All these Humans, belonging to about two dozen star systems, were noble and wise, and eventually assumed the role of guides and teachers of the primitive groups of Humans of the Earth. They all lived together on a continental land separate from the second group, and formed a great, noble and egalitarian civilization that lasted for more than 120,000 years. As time went by, many Human Souls/Selves from their original star systems also came to Earth to incarnate in its humanity.

This third main group of Humans were highly mental beings, creative, artistic and scientific, with refined and graceful physical bodies, and with harmonious and sensitive feeling natures.

It was the second main group of Humans here listed who initiated the changes in attitudes and in understanding that led to "the ancient curse" mentioned in this Stanza VII. A large number of individuals from that group, having come from the same planetary sphere in the solar system, were deeply spiritual in their lives, yet at the same time their spirituality was very materialistic, and they were conquerors in their behavior and militant in all they did. When they started to build their own civilization on Earth — together with those who had come from a second planetary sphere in the solar system and who were entrepreneurial by nature — their character began to change, not just under the influence of the unique evolutionary

Song of the planet but, alas, under the spell of those beings which Stanza IV calls "the Shadows".

Eventually, throughout a number of millennia, this second group of Humans imposed upon themselves and others, in every aspect of their lives, a form of *militant, materialistic and emotional spirituality.* This form of spirituality ended splitting, in their understanding and consciousness, the One Reality that characterizes the entire Universe into what today we call "the natural" and "the super-natural". At the same time, among them elite groups formed who placed themselves as those who were "chosen" and as the mouth-piece of "the super-natural" (i.e. deity).

The effects inflicted by this split *in consciousness* upon the psychology of Humans were so damaging that they are still with us today — the sense that we are separated from The One Source of All; the sense that we fell from grace and that Deity abandoned us; the sense that we are isolated from each other and from all around us, fighting alone to survive in a hostile Universe; the fear of death and of that which is beyond physical existence; the sense that we, and the entire Universe, are just material things, finite and doomed to disappear into nothingness; etc. — all these today-deeply-seated traits in our psychology are the result of that split of the One Reality into the artificial division of "the natural" and "the super-natural". This is "the ancient curse". This is "the twain" that must again become one in our consciousness for us to be whole and able to continue and finish our journey of identity-discovery.

It is important to take notice that the split took place

only in consciousness and not in the factual multi-dimensional nature of Humans, not in their journey of identity-discovery through the various dimensions of Space and Time, not in the nature of Pure Being, and least of all, not in the Oneness that is All. The split has thus been called by the appropriate names of "the Great Heresy of Separateness" and "the Great Illusion" because it is truly a form of mass illusion that, slowly at first but nonetheless progressively, most Humans bought into as the millennia slipped away, to the point that few in every age since then have questioned it.

During the Fifth Age, now climaxing, the development of Mind in Humans has increased the chasm in our consciousness separating "the natural" from the "the super-natural", and both Religion and Science have contributed much to this. But this situation is about to change.

The notion and the recognition of *the One Reality* are going to take a prominent place in our minds and hearts in the decades ahead and as the Sixth Age unfolds. Space, Time and Pure Being Itself are aspects and expressions of The One Source of All — each of them intimately related to the other and having causative effects on each other; each constituted of many levels and dimensions, yet each level and dimension intimately connected to the others with flows of energies and other expressions of Being that truly make of them all *the One Reality.*

There is nothing "natural" in our Universe. There is nothing "super-natural" in our Universe — None of these two are actualities.

What we call "Nature" is neither 'natural' nor 'super-natural', as we understand these terms. Rather, "Nature" is the intimate integration into One Reality of the bio-sphere, the soul-sphere and the spirit-sphere of the Universe.

All is One Reality, One Ocean of Being, in which we live, move and have our being… to which we belong and are an essential component of It… in which we journey to discover progressively that we are actually one with THE SOURCE of that One Reality — never having separated from It, never ceasing to enjoy the countless blessings, abundance and belonging that constitute that One Reality.

We will discover and experience this One Reality when we will stop fighting with each other; when we will cease arguing for who possesses the truth and cease seeking to impose "my truth" upon others; when we will stop condemning differences and diversity; when we will accept that we all are expressions of The One Source of All, each contributing a unique revelation of The One — this is the message of this *Stanza VII,* that we cannot be whole if we are split within and without.

As *Stanza VII* tells us, we need to arrive at a sacred, silent and expectant emptiness, within and without, for us to be ready to discover and experience, again, the One Reality.

In the decades and centuries to come, Religion, in its current state, is going to progressively disappear, to be replaced by a deep Spirituality in which every Human on Earth will feel, know and be aware of the deep connection with the One Reality. But this is not going to be a new form of separation from one another — it will be a recognition of uniqueness, together with a deep attraction to be, to journey and to create together. And thus, we will also feel the need to come together in groups to experience even higher and deeper aspects of that One Reality, higher and deeper than those aspects one can experience alone — this will not be either a new form of worship or of "begging" to a deity for handouts, but it will be an affirmation of our own divinity and a connection with higher aspects of BEING already embodied by Those who are older than us in the journey of identity-discovery and Who dwell in other, more refined spheres of existence. Inspiration, creativity and a widespread transformation of our lives, of the natural world and our entire planet will be the direct consequence of this new form of Spirituality. We will become truly "The Temple re-made" — the Temple of the One Reality where the Mysteries are no longer mysteries but goals to strive towards.

A second main subject addressed by *Stanza VII* refers to changes in the form of Humans, Devas, the natural world and the planet itself, changes which will be concurrent and contributed to by a new pole star for the Earth.

This is a subject that needs to be treated soberly, and with an illuminated mind — as all things forecast and anticipated by the Cycles of Time (i.e. prophesies) should be treated — and without resorting to the usual reactivity of the intellect and the emotions with which many address these types of forecast or anticipation.

Yes, *Stanza VII* tells us that there is going to be a shift of the poles of the Earth and that, instead of the star Polaris, we will have a new pole star. But the Stanza does not provide any information as to the time when this event is going to occur and as to the manner it will happen. Instead, it gives us, through symbolism, two insights about that shift:

It tells us that the shift and the transformation of the Earth, the natural world and the human form will happen when Humans will cease fighting with each other for the usual causes of division that have characterized our lives for ages. It tells us that we will be exhausted in our hearts and minds of the senseless age-old crusades, and that ceasing this fighting will place us in a state of silent, sacred receptivity.

It also tells us that, when we arrive at that inner and outer receptivity, those collectives of Beings who participate in and guide our evolutionary process, together with the energies and sendings of the heavens (i.e. the higher dimensions of BEING), the stars and Sol itself, all of them will come to do their part in that transformation.

Then, analogous to the "leader" or electrical discharge from the ground that calls forth a lightning from a charged atmosphere, a series of transforming events will take place on Earth, the natural world and the human form, including — but not limited to — a shift of the axis of the planet a number of degrees.

Let's comment on 'the silent, sacred emptiness or receptivity', since this is the key for that transformation and shift:

The cosmic energies responsible for the Dawn of the Sixth Age are not going to miraculously change, overnight, all Humans on Earth into some sort of perfected beings. As with all energies coming from other dimensions and levels of existence, they work slowly and they need to be absorbed and consciously integrated into one's being for any benefit to happen. Thus, because of the diversity of evolutionary levels characterizing our humanity, the receptivity, absorption and integration of the energies of the Sixth Age by Humans will be progressive, and it will take some centuries for most to benefit from them — this receptivity, absorption and integration into one's being of the new energies is what *Stanza VII* refers to when telling us about "a sacred emptiness" and a silent expectation.

At the same time, the Stanza tells us that not all Humans have to arrive at that sacred emptiness for the changes to start — it tells us this in the first verse, where it says, "*...and so did many hearts and minds.*" And this means that all that is needed is a critical mass of those who have become receptive to, and are working with the transforming energies of the Sixth Age, for a great transformation to start happening in the human form, in that of the Devas, in the forms of the other kingdoms of Nature, and in the planet itself.

These changes in the form refer to an acceleration of the refinement of the physical forms, compared with the slow changes produced by Evolution — these changes were also addressed in *Stanza VI*, regarding the rising of "the Dragon Fire", or the activation of the "dark swirls" of Matter in the substances of the planet.

Because of this refinement in our bodies, for example, we will be able to perceive etheric and astral levels of existence through the normal five senses, and will be able communicate with those who had passed over or with those who are returning into incarnation. This refinement will also allow us to communicate telepathically with each other, to communicate through feeling with animals, and to progressively diminish our susceptibility to diseases of all types until perfect health will become a common occurrence.

Together with all these developments in Humans, the natural world and the planet will also be able to absorb and use cosmic energies that until now just passed through without leaving any benefit. It will be this enhanced capacity of the Earth to absorb and use those new energies that will prompt a shift of its axis, a redressing of the continental lands, and having a new pole star.

These changes and transformation have already started! — slowly but surely, and none can stop them.

These changes don't have to be catastrophic. They can happen with a disruption of the human civilization and of the natural world that we can cope with as they happen. On the other hand, these changes could also be turbulent, with a great disruption for our lives and the natural world. It all depends on how soon, or not, we will let go of "the age-old crusades" and arrive at the sacred emptiness within us and without us. The fact is, the energies of the Sixth Age are and will keep coming regardless of what we do with them. They will keep coming asking us, and applying pressure on us, to let go of the old and 'be more'.

A final note here on this subject to ponder on:

Having a new pole star is not just an astronomical event. It also means, for the Earth, to be able to receive new energies necessary for the next evolutionary step for its bio-sphere and soul-sphere. For us Humans, it also means that we have a new "North" in our existence and journey of identity-discovery — that new "North" is 'the One Reality', and so the beneficent energies of the new pole star will help us realize. And this re-alignment of our hearts and minds and consciousness will allow us to rejoice and to join in the Song of creation of The Powers, the stars and those other collectives of Beings who travel with us:

The Temple has been remade!

...

Rejoice, Humans and Angels! – Join in the Song!

★

The People of the New

Black and Blue, and Red and Yellow, and Brown and even White, all had come from One Light. Crystal-clear once they all had been clad. Yet, Time in its twists and the pains of the heart had altered their attire. So masked and hidden their starlight now was, they all came to believe poles apart they were in their like and paths — even though every night the symphony of the stars sang to them otherwise.

The New Day transformed that. The rising Sun phased their timelines into one, and it shone its light deep inside through their colored masks. Unclad they all felt with its light, and many rushed to hide while others to mar that which was revealed by the daylight. But the Morning would have none of that — in the light they had to face their stars!

Before long, though, one by one recognized the beauty of their lights, and together they came to restore with their colors a One Light new in its kind. And this was the sign the stars and The Powers had awaited in patience and foresight — the Prodigal Pilgrim was now on their way back to The One!

And it came to pass. Hand in hand, and facing the Light, and with a clear mind knowing the want of their heart, their lives Humans re-made in the image of that. To reveal The One in a new Light was now their path, and with music and song and the beauty that comes from the heart they were ready to do that.

And thus the Song of the Earth to the stars and the heavens the New Ones rose to new heights. And with this The Powers could now proceed with their Plans — Time and Space were about to take a new path, unlike those they had trodden so far.

* * *

Commentary

The message contained in the beautiful symbolism of this *Stanza VIII* is plain and direct, and difficult to miss. It first addresses the mysterious origin of *Diversity* in Humans, revealing its causes. Then, it tells us that Diversity has done its work, and that now is the time to return to that unity that characterized us before our journey through Time and Space began. And at the end, it tells us what is going to happen once we bridge all divisions and start working together.

Let's comment on these points.

The subject of *Diversity* is, without doubt, one of the most pressing subjects calling our attention in the present times, to the point that in every land and in every nation people today cannot ignore its reality. This fact in itself tells us that the Dawn of the Sixth Age is now with us.

But Diversity *in its essence* is not about race, gender, cultural background, religious persuasion, economic wellbeing, education, evolutionary development, and the like. These all are effects in Time and in Space of a deeper, *planned* Diversity.

As the Stanza reminds us, in the beginning we were, in our essence, One Light — colorless and crystal-clear. However, something happened that split this One Light in a spectrum of colors; then, as Time went by and as our experiences as form-bound beings mounted, each of those colors, in turn, split into other spectra of colors. And this is where we find ourselves today, at the furthermost place from our origin and at the greatest degree of diversity as Humans — our only path now is to turn around and start the journey of return to unity.

In the Stanza, the symbolism of the expression "One Light" means that, before we started journeying through Time and Space, we were Pure Being, one sole *expression* of The One Source of All — endowed with all the divine Aspects and Attributes of The One, but at the same time unaware of the extent and reach of those Powers and Qualities. We were like a child who is born as a music prodigy but who has never composed, played or sung anything.

Every expression of The One Source of All — and there are countless of them — is sourced (i.e. launched into Be-ing) to enrich the Universe and make of it 'more'. Yet, to add beauty to this grand symphony of creation, each expression of The One is free to choose how it will proceed to do that. And it was thus that we, Cosmic Humanity, were sourced as One Ray of Light to enrich the Universe in a unique way, a way that we ourselves would choose. And we chose, but we chose something seldom chosen — we chose to make of ourselves *diverse*, to make of our One Ray a spectrum of rays as we traveled through Time and Space, learning more about our potential, with the goal of making of the richness of *'Unity in Diversity'* our contribution to the Universe.

And so the path we have chosen is in itself, both, an effect of that *planned* Diversity and a means to become more diverse. We planned timelines that were diverse in themselves, with some of us starting first the journey of identity-discovery, others starting somewhat later, and still others much later — and this explains the diversity of evolutionary states in humanity that we experience on Earth. We also planned to experience Diversity on all the levels and dimensions offered by Space — and this explains the multi-dimensional constitution of our form as Space-bound beings, with energies and substances that span from the less refined and most dense at the Matter level to the most refined at the Spirit level.

We are thus not only diverse as a collective, but also each of us is diverse within oneself — yet, this diversity 'within' and 'without' is not a handicap or a limitation but is our *wealth*.

All the outer, perceivable expressions of Diversity — race, gender, culture, religious persuasion, economic wellbeing, education, evolutionary development, etc. — are just that, expressions of our accumulated psychological, mental and spiritual *wealth* as One Humanity, a wealth we can assess and access only through the eyes of love, goodwill and understanding.

The second point addressed by *Stanza VIII* — that Diversity has done its work and now is the time to return to unity — explains the historical moment we have been living in the past few centuries and that is climaxing in the present time.

The overall message of the *"Stanzas of The Dawn"* is that we, as One Humanity, are now living a dual moment in Time: the ending of a stage in our journey of identity-discovery (the Fifth Age), and the beginning of a stage 'unlike' those we have traveled so far (the Sixth Age) — 'unlike', because it will take us to the stars and beyond, and because it will require of us to get in touch with our deepest essence.

The great lesson of the stages we have traveled so far has been for each of us to discover *oneself* and the extent of *one's* possibilities and potential.

The great lesson ahead of us in the new stage is to discover *ourselves* and the extent of *our* possibilities and potential.

The Light of the New Dawn, which we have been living since right before the Renaissance, has brought to our attention, progressively but surely, the fact of Diversity. The discovery and the spread of knowledge regarding all the lands and peoples of the Earth; the widespread contact with all the many peoples and cultures we now enjoy; the unveiling of the great diversity that characterizes the natural world revealed by science; the advances in traveling and communication which reduced the distances between each other to a minimum; the universality of opportunities of education for all; the discovery of the Earth's place and her relationships in Space; etc. — all these advances have been possible because of the Light of the New Dawn; they have been and are the result of a planned intention to make of us, individually and collectively, aware of the richness of our Diversity as the One Humanity of planet Earth.

And now that the Morning has broken, the realization and the attraction to come together as One Humanity are growing in our hearts and minds like a fire impossible to stop. The movements everywhere towards democratic participation in government that have characterized the past 250 years; the many coordinated efforts to heal the divisions within societies, between peoples and among nations; the intense preoccupation everywhere with the economy and with finding just and fair ways that benefit all; the quiet revolution in spirituality, which is rejecting and leaving behind the tyranny of dogmas, doctrines and religious impositions, and which is embracing all human beings, the natural world and divinity as One; the growing attraction for traveling to other lands, to meet other peoples and to experience other cultures; etc. — all these collective aspirations, movements and efforts have come to be because the Morning of the New Day has already broken, reminding us that it is time to make of the many 'colors' a One Light.

We are, thus, already on our way *from the many to the One* — from *'separation in Diversity'* to a *'Unity in Diversity'* — and nothing and no one can stop this from happening, since it is the will of our collective Soul, a will supported by the Cycles of Time.

As for what the future has for us once we will arrive at a worldwide coordinated effort to live and work together as One Humanity, *Stanza VIII* tells us that, then and only then, events will fast unfold that will facilitate for us to achieve those goals, and which will reveal to us powers, qualities and insights we as yet don't realize we have.

Not every Human on Earth has to come simultaneously to the point of wanting and of working towards togetherness. What is needed is a critical mass and a more focused intention and efforts in the direction of *accepting ourselves as One Humanity,* together with taking concrete steps towards re-organizing our lives — as individuals, societies and nations — based on that acceptance. Then, certain collectives of Beings from the stars, and Those Powers Who guide and travel with us the journey of identity-discovery, will release certain energies upon the Earth and will unveil in us and in the natural world powers and qualities we didn't know we have.

This is our path ahead, the promise of the New Day, the message of *Stanza VIII.* Suffering, lack and separation will fade away from our consciousness and lives. They have already finished their work of teaching us Diversity. From now on, our journey is just a remembering of our essential nature as One Light and of using together for the greatest good of All the richness each has learned.

★

Stanza IX

The Magic of the Heart

Tossed from here to there, since the start life had been that for Humans and Earth. The Two Origins hadn't had that which could bring Them together as one. And Humans and Earth's creatures had danced at their tune without regard. Yet the Morning Star brought to their hearts renewed strength to do otherwise — and with this, One was about to arise whose Magic was going to give a new task to the Two who came before Time.

An outpost of The One, a door to the stars, a revealer of Life, a bridge across Time, the way to the Gods, the Path to neither here nor there but Beyond — these and the like are in the Heart. Yet, Humans for ages remember not that, their eyes set on Death and its wants.

"Time and Space veiled your face,
making of it a beast in the field.

Prey for Death then you became.
Yet, Life isn't there –
Look within you and find your true face.
The Heart of THE ONE *awaits for you there."*

— So the Morning Star sang to the many of Earth, sending her harmonies to all seeking hearts.

None could ignore the might of her Song — She was the Dawn, the Harbinger and the New Sun made into one. Transforming, her harmonies all felt in their hearts, directing their eyes to THAT to Whom none had beheld since the fall — And lo! soon after that, the Heart of THE ONE all beheld within them, and with this the beast an Angel became.

A New Earth and many new stars were about to shine because of the Heart. And with this THE ONE could now descend from on High to walk the seas and the lands — the Heart in its Magic had planned on that. Humans were now the Angel, the God and The One made into ONE!

★ ★ ★

Commentary

The first observation we can make of this beautiful *Stanza IX* is that its central theme is "the Heart" and its role in the journey of identity-discovery, along Time and Space, we Humans are engaged in. In the Commentary of *Stanza VI,* some observations were made about "the Magic of the Heart", with the emphasis on

'Magic' as the creative power natural to Humans to transform Time and Space, and to free themselves from their clutches. Here, *Stanza IX* enjoins us to give attention to 'the Heart' itself as our true essential nature.

What is "the Heart"? To what exactly are the *"Stanzas of The Dawn"* referring when speaking of "the Heart"?

Before answering that question, it is worth noticing that we all use regularly expressions such as… 'I feel it in my heart'… 'My heart tells me'… 'The love of my heart'… 'It feels right (or wrong) in my heart'… etc. — To what are we referring when we use the word 'heart' in those expressions?

Obviously, both the Stanzas and we use the expressions "the Heart" and "the heart" in a symbolic way; yet both are pointing to the same Reality… both associate the word with Love, Wisdom and Goodness… and none is actually referring to the physical organ of the heart. The only difference between the use of that expression by the Stanzas and how we use it in our daily lives is that "the Heart" in the *"Stanzas of The Dawn"* refers to the fullness of that Reality to which the word points, while we use the expression "the heart" mostly unconsciously and without a full understanding of what we refer to — although, this doesn't make us wrong in its use.

To understand that Reality which the expression "the Heart" points to, we need to review our true nature and constitution as Humans — which the Stanza describes for us when it tells us that each of us is *a 'beast' who becomes an Angel, plus a God, plus The One.* Then the Stanza goes further and states that, though we are three in appearance (that is, in Time and Space), we are ONE in our Essence.

Most religious theologies, doctrines, scriptures and teachings fall short of presenting the true picture of the human being as *a triune being,* sourced, vitalized and directed by *One Essence.* In addition, modern science hasn't been able, yet, to go beyond the physical body in its understanding of the human being. The reason for these limitations has been the lack of development of the human mind and the consequent lack of refinement of the human brain; lacks which limit the perception and understanding of the more subtle aspects of the One Reality, and hence of the most subtle aspects of the human being — to this, the illusory split of the One Reality into "the natural" and "the super-natural" has also contributed greatly, creating confusion and misplaced emphases. This lack of mental and nervous-system development also accounts for the unsatisfactory, distorted, materialistic and inadequate presentation of Divinity that religions offer. This situation is now changing with the arrival of Dawn and the breaking of the Sixth Age.

Moved by the Cycles of Time, the evolutionary process is doing its work, and Humans are rapidly developing their mind in all its aspects, at the same time that their nervous system is becoming more refined and more sensitive in its processes, perceptions and receptivity to subtle energies and states of Being — this, of course, doesn't happen in one incarnation but along a number of them. Nonetheless, in the present and in the decades and centuries to come, Humans are becoming and are going to become more aware of those Energies and "Presences" which now we call by the vague terms of 'Devas', 'Angels', 'Soul', 'Spirit', 'God', 'Divinity'.

These advances in our development as Humans, aided and accelerated by the energies arriving with the Dawn, will revolutionize our understanding of ourselves, of the natural world, and of Divinity and the Universe, with the consequent beneficial impact on our minds and bodies, on our ways of living, on our health and on our creations.

This *Stanza IX* reminds us that, as Humans, we are a mental~feeling~vital being expressing through a physical form — i.e. a persona or, as the Stanza describes it: 'the beast' who is destined to transform or alchemize itself into an Angel. We are also, at the same time, 'a God' or Soul, whose nature is Love and Creative Power, and whose entire drive is to use that Love and Power for the greatest good of all. Yet, we are likewise 'Something' so great and exalted that only a few Humans along history have discovered It and embodied It... 'Something' which human languages and the works of the mind cannot grasp... 'Something' which only the combined identities of the Soul and the refined persona (i.e. 'the beast' transformed into the Angel) can perceive and eventually identify with — that 'Something' is Spirit, The One, whose expressions are omnipotency, omnipresence and omniscience.

Yet, there is more to us, and the Stanza also reminds us of that — that our identity doesn't end there, with those three.

An Essence — immutable, infinite and eternal, and beyond all conception — gives existence, purpose and motion to the three we are during our journey of identity-discovery in Time and Space. An ESSENCE which the Stanza refers to in the verses: *'THAT to Whom none had beheld since the fall'*... *'the Heart of THE ONE'*... *'THE ONE could now descend from on High to walk the seas and the lands'*... and ultimately with the simple expression, *'the Heart'*.

It doesn't serve us to speculate on that ESSENCE which is our truest Identity. We still need to make of 'the beast' the Angel; we still need to become the Soul-infused persona; and then, we still need to reach out, with that purified identity, to Spirit before we can experience the three as ONE — that ESSENCE.

Nonetheless, regardless of the stage in our journey of identity-discovery, we all sense THE PRESENCE of that ESSENCE, we all are attracted to IT, and we all know in our deepest feelings that we are of IT. To IT we reach out with our prayers and in our meditations. To IT we cry for help in our deepest moments of sorrow. We contact IT when we are grateful for the abundance ceaselessly surrounding us. We also feel IT when we feel the blessing presence of Nature all around us. And ultimately, our awareness of IT blossoms and grows in us when we love 'all that breathes and has existence' without waiting for anything in return.

Thus, this *Stanza IX* enjoins us to ponder on, and to give attention in our lives to 'the Heart' — it tells us that the key to the entire mystery of our existence, of our identity, and of our destiny, is found in 'the Heart'.

It is not uncommon, when one becomes consciously

aware that we are on a journey of identity-discovery (by whatever name we may call this journey), to be attracted and to give a lot of attention to writings, teachings, scriptures, and in general to presentations of that journey made by others.

However, it is only when one sees through the fact that all of them are just the opinions and the perspectives of others, that one will turn the attention *within*… that one will start to observe oneself (one's thoughts, one's feelings, one's words, one's actions)… that one will start to consciously use love, goodwill and understanding in life. It is then that one will make a faster and a more rounded progress along the journey… it is then that one will begin the process of redeeming 'the beast' to its true nature, an Angel… it is then that one will continue to become, next, the Soul or timeless Self, and later Spirit itself so that identification with that ESSENCE which sourced us can happen.

In the following words from the Morning Star, this *Stanza IX* reminds us of that imperative need to look and search *within* to discover our true nature:

> *"Time and Space veiled your face,*
> *making of it a beast in the field.*
> *Prey for Death then you became.*
> *Yet, Life isn't there –*
> *Look within you and find your true face.*
> *The Heart of THE ONE awaits for you there."*

*

Stanza X

The Symphony of Time

The Point born from THE ONE, a Line It became. Yet, such was Its glee and Its thrust, with a spin into a Spiral It transformed Itself. To and fro Its attraction grew for that which wasn't Its own, bending and adding more twists to Its flow. And with this, the Two Origins were drawn to Its dancing and singing, powerless to the charm of Its coming and going.

Circles, squares and spheres, and others like these, took shape from Its coming and going. And again the Two Origins could not but follow, adding color and weight to the Symphony of light and sound the Point sang on Its own.

At each turn and a flow – order, dimension and purpose the Point gave to that which wasn't Its own. And in each ordered sphere that so came to exist, Orders of Beings It left as Its own, to flow on their own and so add their songs to the Song born as a point, a line and a spiral.

First was the point charged to flow, then patterns had come directed to sail on the Origins' ocean, to end in the forms known to all whose fate takes them on the journey from here to There.

And such was the song the Harbinger sang as the Morning Star rose high in the sky. It was directed to those whose heart was awake and whose mind soared the heights. Left in the Luminous Sea by the Teachers of Old, it sang of the origin of all things and beings, and of their journey through Time and Space towards that waiting Horizon the Harbinger held open to all.

✶ ✶ ✶

Commentary

This *Stanza X* is deeply symbolic and not so easy to associate with its central idea — *Time.* Nonetheless, using geometry, the Stanza does describe the origin of Time and the consequent appearance of that which we call 'Space'.

More evident in the Stanza is, however, a universal and powerful formula for creation — for true Magic, the magic of Thought.

Stanza X is also a good example of the timelessness of the teachings left in the Sea of Light — i.e. in the universal Light of Akasha — by the Ancient Teachers.*

During the Fourth Age this Stanza was taught to the

---

* See Commentary to *Stanza I.*

advanced Humans of the time — who were less developed in their minds and in the use of feeling than most Humans now when the Fifth Age is ending and the Sixth Age is dawning. Unfortunately, in those older times a number of them interpreted the Stanza as a raw magical formula for the manifestation of material things — interpretation that fed in them rampant desire, and that ended in a tragic misuse of the forces of Nature. This distortion was one of the main factors that led to the great war between the Forces of Light and the Forces of Darkness, which ended with the demise of the last civilization of that Age by 'drowning desire' or 'water'.

Such was the misuse of the formula in that Age that during the Fifth Age *Stanza X* was not revealed to Humans, waiting for the development of their minds and their hearts. During the Sixth Age now arriving, however, when 'the heart' in Humans is awakening and when the use of the higher faculties of Mind will become a common occurrence, the symbolism of the Stanza will be studied in its more subtle interpretations — which was the intention of the Ancient Teachers in Their task to foster the journey of identity-discovery in Humans.

The intended interpretations of this *Stanza X* start with obtaining an understanding, as far as one can, of the 'Two Origins' and of the creative process They initiated, and which we currently experience as 'the Universe'. Once we gain some understanding of this, we can correlate it with the creative power that each of us is and for which one is fully responsible. And this is the approach we are going to take in this Commentary.

Three main ideas are contained in *Stanza X:* first, 'the Point' as an expression of THE ONE, and the nature of Its motions; second, the omnipresence of the Two Origins; and third, the creation resulting from the interaction between the Point and the Two Origins.

Let's comment on these ideas in their order.

Space, as we know it, thanks to the advances in modern science, hasn't existed as such since the beginning of our present Universe. No, Space is a later appearance. The Perennial Wisdom teaches that the first to appear as emanations from the Absolute Causeless Cause — i.e. The One Source of All — were *two Primordial Forces.* With our present mental development, these two Forces or Emanations we can discern and understand in various ways — *Light* and *Darkness* is one of them, yet not as 'good' and 'evil' but as *'the Impulse to Be'* and *'the Impulse to not-Be'.**

These two Primordial Forces are the *'Two Origins'* to whom this and others of the *"Stanzas of The Dawn"* refer.

Some may confuse the Two Origins with the more familiar duality of Spirit~Matter. However, this duality is

---

* *'The Impulse to Be'* and *'the Impulse to not-Be'* are the root of all perceived and experienced dualities, including that one which religion on Earth has so much misrepresented — so called 'good' and 'evil' — 'misrepresented' since neither 'good' nor 'evil' exist as such. Only that root duality exists, and only for the period of this Universe.

a later appearance in our Universe and can only be applied to the experience in Time and in Space undertaken by certain Orders of Beings, including us Humans and the many beings of the natural world that we know of.

What these two Primordial Forces — *the Impulse to Be* and *the Impulse to not-Be* — created for themselves when They came into existence was something not so easy to picture with our minds. To start with, the Two Origins didn't interact with each other directly; there was no attraction between them, and their creation was an inchoate amalgamation of mighty forces charged with repulsion and lacking order and direction; and, of course, no forms at all were created. For the sake of this commentary we could call the product of Their creative work by the term 'Primordial Space', though the word 'space' is too generous since there wasn't a 'space' at all — Theirs was a pure existence devoid of locality and dimensionality, intelligent but impulsive, and lacking in the realization of 'a building potential'. Energy, Force, Light, Electricity and Magnetism, as we perceive and know them today, didn't exist at all, nor had Time appeared either. Theirs was, and is, a primeval BEINGNESS as a precursor of BEING.

Later, when those two Primordial Forces settled into a dynamic equilibrium, *a Third Force* or *Emanation* from The One Source of All came into existence. This Third Force was, and is, of a different essence and nature to the Two Origins; and with our present mental development we can also discern it and understand it from various perspectives — one of them is as *The Great Archi-*

tect and Builder of the Universe, as it was called in ancient times, or more appropriate for the Sixth Age, as *The Thinker.*

This Third Force or Emanation, The Thinker, is 'THE ONE' referred to in the first verse of this *Stanza X* — THE ONE from which 'the Point' (i.e. Thought) was born.

It was The Thinker who gave and gives order, direction and purpose to the interaction of the Two Origins. It is The Thinker who made and makes of Their primeval BEINGNESS true BEING. It is The Thinker who drew and draws out from the Two Origins a true creative, intelligent interaction. It is The Thinker who is responsible for the appearance of Time and Space as we know them, with all the myriads of Orders of Beings and the many forms they create and experience.

Let's study more The Thinker, since It is the key player in this Stanza — besides, as we are going to see, The Thinker is our essential Identity… It is WHO each of us truly *is.*

The Thinker is, in essence, Pure Being, the Absolute Self, Pure Identity — forever an outsider to the Universe itself, yet with a boundless power to direct and shape the interaction between the Two Origins.

The Thinker's contact with the Two Origins is represented in the Stanza by 'the Point'.

Again, it was the action of The Thinker upon Primordial Space that transformed it into Space as we know it — with all its Orders of Beings, energies, light-fields, forces and ordering laws, producing stars, galaxies, super-clusters, the many dimensions beyond these, and the many forms and processes in them.

But before Space became the ordered system that it is today, something happened first: *Time* appeared! And the Stanza reminds us of this when it tells us of the motions of the Point as 'a Line' and as 'a Spiral' — motions which ended creating complex patterns of attraction.

Interpreting what the Stanza tells us using geometry, and to better grasp the nature of Time and how it precedes Space, let's delve into the way The Thinker works — let's grasp Its role as 'the Third Force' in this Universe of ours.

The Thinker, using Its own essence — *Pure Identity* — and drive — *the Power of Imagining* — casts images of Identity, or reflections of Itself, or 'Points', upon the ocean of interaction between the Two Origins… an infinite number of them, each one different from the others, ceaselessly and with such a rhythm and such a harmony that they constitute a true Song of songs. Through each of these images of Identity — which are the many Orders of Beings of the Universe — The Thinker interacts intimately with the two Primordial Forces, to show Them the countless possibilities of what They too can be.

Each of these images of Identity starts as a 'Point', who, by design, follows a journey of identity-discovery, a journey which is for the benefit of the Two Origins — as well as a path for 'the Point' to return to its originating Source, The Thinker. The product of this journey is, invariably, states of Consciousness/Awareness — series of them, harmonically related to each other and to the states of Consciousness/Awareness created by the journeys of the other many 'Points'. In the process, the two Primordial Forces are compelled to follow this journey, to contribute to it, to partake of it, to explore it, and thus to experience those states of Consciousness/Awareness.

The Thinker's Song of songs, formed by the countless journeys of Identity It creates, is that which each of The Thinker's projected Identities — the many Orders of Beings — experience as *Time.*

> Thus, from the perspective of the Perennial Wisdom, *Time* is not the passing of days and years, or the progression of spatial events, one after the other. Time is, instead, the rhythmic, harmonic and multi-dimensional journey of identity-discovery experienced by the images of Itself The Thinker casts into existence out of Its own Essence; journey which creates and is experienced as states or spheres of Consciousness.

But there is more to Time. It is this countless number of journeys of identity-discovery, and the countless number of states or spheres of Consciousness they so create, that gives order, locality, dimensionality and direction to the interaction between the Two Origins. And the result of this process between Time and the Two Origins is *Space* as we know it, with its order and its energies, and its forces and its light-fields, in which myriads of galaxies, multi-dimensional levels of existence, and all beings and things take form.

Thus, in the process of creation Time appears first, and Space follows it, as an effect.

More precisely, first is The Thinker, picturing or imagining an expression of Itself (i.e. the Point, a Thought). Then, The Thinker casts Its image-creation (i.e. the reflection of Itself endowed with a particular Identity) upon the ocean of existence (i.e. the interaction of the Two Origins). And the result is an Identity who journeys through that ocean of existence, impressing motion, direction and purpose to it, and by so doing, creating its own Time (or timeline). Lastly, what is perceived of that journey of identity-discovery and of the reaction of the Two Origins to it, is what we call Space.

Time is, then, a creation and an experience *in consciousness* exclusive to the Identities projected by The Thinker (i.e. Selves or Mind-Souls). Energy, in its many modalities, which is of Space, doesn't experience Time.

More specifically, it is the Identities projected by The Thinker (i.e. our Selves and the many other Orders of Beings) who impress their flow and changing states of consciousness/awareness upon that which They appropriate, touch and use from the ocean of existence during their journeys of identity-discovery, and thus create Space. And to make this process closer, it is in fact *us* who create Time as we go and who, by doing that, create and attract to us the energies and forms we want to experience, and how we want to experience them.

To grasp these ideas on Time and Space takes some pondering and abstract thinking (that is, non-materializing thinking) since, evidently, they don't match the notions on Time and Space held by contemporary Science, nor the notions of Religion about us, Humans, and about Divinity. However, we need to notice that our present perception and understanding of Time and Space are based on our current understanding of life — which is materialistic and limited to that which we perceive with our physical senses and their extensions, the instruments of Science, and which we interpret with a mind that concretizes all thinking into material representations. All this is the product of the Fifth Age; it is the product of the development of mind attained during the Fifth Age. Yet, nothing is wrong with how our minds work today. It is just a stage on the journey.

We also need to keep in mind that Science and Religion, as are also Philosophy and Art, in their current state are not more than crude tools to delve into the mysteries encountered along our journey of identity-discovery at the stage we are at. They too need to change, expand and become more refined, and will change and expand and become more refined as we become 'more', as we discover 'more' of us with every step ahead.

As the Sixth Age unfolds, a growing and large number of Humans will develop their extended senses (capable of perceiving higher forms of energy and higher states of Being), and their minds will be able to deal with abstract (non-concretizing) and exalted thinking. These developments will make of the creative process (true Magic, true Thinking) an everyday reality for each of us. It will then become a daily experience for most the fact that we do create Time and Space. It will become a daily experience the fact that every creation, and every being and thing in existence (including our persona) starts with a Thought (the Point), a thought that, as we build it, creates its own timeline (the Line), and that we cast into the ocean of manifestation by our very desire to make of it an experience (the Spiral).

Those developments of our senses and our minds will not happen overnight. They will take decades and centuries to happen. Nonetheless, the main reason this *Stanza X* is now made public, at the Dawn of the Sixth Age, is that it has a direct application in the lives of those who today seek the Light — those who seek to 'be more'. The Stanza enjoins us to grasp the fact that life for each of us is a journey of identity-discovery, that each of us creates its own journey as one travels, and that each of us is directly responsible for all the experiences one has along that journey.

The Stanza enjoins us to see our bodies, our relationships and our daily experiences as our own creation — a creation that follows a clear and a precise process: first is an idea followed by the thought that builds it, then is the projection of that thought in a specific direction or goal, followed by the infusion to it of an actual desire to see it into manifested existence. Once we follow this process, nothing and no one can arrest our experiencing that creation. On the contrary, the great ocean of Primordial Forces will rush to comply with our fiat.

Thus, controlling our thinking in all our waking moments is the central key for becoming the masters of the experiences we want to have during the journey of identity-discovery we are traveling. Seeing our lives as a creation one is responsible for — and not as the product of circumstances beyond our control, or of others' doings — is what the Stanza enjoins us to acknowledge. But the Stanza doesn't end with this exhortation. It gives us one more clue. It tells us that the more we love all beings and things, without waiting for anything in return, and the more our mind focuses on that which is uplifting, positive and joyful, the easier and faster one becomes in fullness The Thinker, the Creator, the true Magician. The Stanza gives us this clue in the words:

> And such was the song the Harbinger sang as the Morning Star rose high in the sky. It was directed to those whose heart was awake and whose mind soared the heights.

★

The Path to
the Farthest Horizon

Lonesome for ages their path had been, refusing to follow the tried and tested ways, and discarding memories weighing down their march ahead. So set their eyes were on their trail, that what had prompted them to such a fate no longer was in them.

Yet, unbeknown to them, the stars remembered for them the purpose of their going.

For eons ahead they went, at times crossing valleys and summits lit by heavens' lights, yet it was most times across the dark and dreary netherworld they dragged themselves on. No place was hidden or sealed to their going. And in so doing, the fallen, the forgotten, the forsaken, the unwanted, the unknown, and all those whose path was as lonely as their own, they gathered along their going — near their hearts where warmth was always glowing.

> Yet, unbeknown to them, the Song of a new order of galaxies of stars were they forging.

Those who with them traveled, as blind as them they were on the reason for their going. Yet, with them they shared the attraction for the hidden and forbidden, and their love for the fallen, the forgotten, the forsaken, the unwanted and the unknown.

Born higher than the mighty Archangels of the Heavens had they been, though from early on the fate of the fallen and forgotten had they chosen — their cries of pain drawing them to those remote corners of existence where loneliness, oblivion and despair had made their home.

> Yet, unbeknown to them, as a beacon alight in the dark of night, their origin the Archangels of the Heavens kept for them.

And so it came to be, as all things must come to be, after aeons of so going, that at the darkest place, when no light was left and their hearts had run out of strength, at long last they rose their eyes to the pageantry of the Heavens, who lost no time in reminding them of the purpose for their going and of the mighty light and love their hearts shone far and wide across the stars.

And it was then, at last, that — together with the cosmic vessel who for ages had carried them along the ocean of existence, and with the stars who with them had kept their vigil, and gathering the fallen, the forgotten, the forsaken, the unwanted and the unknown closer to their hearts — they set sail to the farthest Horizon, beyond Space and Time, a Horizon foreseen by them at the moment when from THE ONE they came into existence.

*　*　*

Commentary

Stanza XI is, perhaps, the most deeply HUMAN of all the "*Stanzas of The Dawn*". Its overall theme is '*the mystery of Suffering*' and its intimate association with the uniqueness of the path trodden by us, Earth Humans.

Only a handful of spheres in the Seven Galaxies (of which our galaxy is one) follow evolutionary processes in which pain and suffering play a role for the Orders of Beings there journeying. It is very difficult for us, Earth Humans, and perhaps unbelievable, to conceive and accept that the entire thrust and design of the Universe in which we live is geared towards *JOY* — that all the laws and processes of this Universe are designed to provide and foster joy, fulfillment, ever-expanding freedom from limitation, abundance, illumination and, ultimately, bliss.

Suffering plays such a predominant role in our existence that we haven't yet truly acknowledged and accepted that *The One Source of All is Love*. Although 2,000 years have passed since the Great Teacher came to show us the actuality of that Love, we still don't accept it as a fact in our lives. The reality in our psychology is other — living and suffering go together, in spite of all the tricks and measures we may design and take to bypass suffering.

This *Stanza XI* not only explains to us the reason for the Earth being "the Sphere of Suffering", but it also shows us the path out of Suffering.

Let's then comment on this theme:

There is something so unique in our psychological nature and life thrust as Earth Humans — 'unique' when compared with the many other Humanities and self-conscious Orders of Beings elsewhere in the Seven Galaxies — that it is hard for us to even see it as such. And that uniqueness we can describe in this way:

> We are attracted to conceive and think that which hasn't been imagined or thought before... We are attracted to live on the fringes of existence... We are attracted to explore the boundaries beyond the known... We are trailblazers... We dislike rules and laws... We love freedom from constraints... We like to bypass and defeat the established order of things... We like to explore that which is hidden, forbidden and unknown... We defend our own way and are proud of it... And, *at the same time,* our hearts cannot but fall in love with those who suffer, with those who are lonely, with those who are the outsiders, with those who are the forgotten, the

forsaken and the unwanted — all of this is *us*, in spite that at times we don't acknowledge it or try to forget it!

Torchbearers of Sacrificial Will and Compassion — so the stars call us.

And it is this unique path we have chosen that explains *the mystery of Suffering.*

Suffering is thus the result of 'going against the grain'; it is the result of turning our backs to the normal flow of the Universe, resulting in challenges, friction and disappointments at every step we take. But here is something regarding our path that may astonish many, and so the Stanza reminds us: In our very beginning we freely chose to turn our backs to the normal flow of the Universe! We knew we were going to incur suffering, yet we nonetheless went ahead, and keep going ahead, along the path we chose! — and all because of Love. We heard then, and keep hearing today, the cry of the fallen, the forgotten, the forsaken, the unwanted and the unknown, and our hearts cannot but go to them.

Here is a note of encouragement to remember when suffering seeks to overwhelm us:

When the Great Teacher told us the parable of the Prodigal Son, He reminded us of what The One Source of All (i.e. "the Father") thought of our "rebellion" and journey to the fringes of existence. He reminded us that "the Father" was more pleased with the Prodigal Son than with the Son who had remained at home!

A more pertinent question than 'the why of suffering' is, therefore, the question of the existence of the fallen, the forgotten, the forsaken, the unwanted and the unknown. How in a Universe of Love, with all its laws and processes designed to foster Joy, can they exist? Who are they? Where do they come from? What happened to them to be in such a state? Where are they now? How can we hear their cry? Are we the only ones who hear their cry?

With these questions we are seeking to penetrate into a much deeper mystery than the mystery of Suffering, a mystery that nonetheless affects us… a mystery that deals with realms of existence of a nature unlike anything known to us and to many others in the stars… a mystery that deals with Orders of Beings of a nature for which we have no conception and whose entire life thrust isn't to become 'more' but to become 'less' and to 'shy away' from The One Source of All.

The impediment we currently have to penetrate into, and to truly understand this mystery of the fallen, the forgotten, the forsaken, the unwanted and the unknown, is that our journey of identity-discovery *as Humans on this Earth* is in the nature of a training or schooling process during which we are learning to express love and to assist those who experience such a fate. And to do this learning — that is, to actualize in us that we are truly Love and Compassion, even in the midst of the most challenging circumstances — *we split ourselves into groups that would embody and act out each of those experiences so that we could learn with each other*. In addition, we populated the bio-sphere of the planet with groups of beings, specially in the animal king-dom, who would also draw from us Love and Compassion as we all journey together to make of the Earth a showcase of Love, Harmony and Beauty.

We are so focused on this learning immersion that we forgot the greater purpose for which we are learning — which is, to truly love and to reach out with wisdom, later on our journey, into those 'unlit' realms where the fallen, the forgotten, the forsaken, the unwanted and the unknown are cut off from the Light. For this mission we will be ready once we finish our journey of identity-discovery on this Earth, when we will 'be more' than Human, when we will truly be *Torchbearers of Sacrificial Will and Compassion* and *Dragons of Wisdom.*

Our journey as Humans on this Earth has been, to say the least, challenging, yet it has been a great learning experience regarding Love. We have experienced with each other, at times, the heights of harmony, together-ness and caring; though many more times, the lows of uncaring, rejection and disharmony — and still, we have kept going! Things are changing however, and our schooling is coming to its end — mostly, because the cycles allotted by the Cosmic Clock to our school-ing on this Earth are coming to their end, and it is for this reason that the Sixth and the Seventh Ages are go-ing to be for 'gathering' and 'demonstrating' the fruits of our schooling, and for returning to our original unity. Then, after that, our real mission begins!

During the past few centuries, and right now, most of us on this Earth are awakening to the reality of 'togeth-erness'... of One Humanity... of One Planet... of caring for each other… of not leaving anyone behind — and this awakening is happening everywhere, regardless of culture, historical background, ethnicity, religion, political persuasion, evolutionary development, and any of those artificial conditions and superficial traits we have created for ourselves. We are truly well on our way to make a real experience for all the fact that we are One Humanity and One Planet.

Yes, there is no doubt that we are seeing today the worst in Humans. But we are also seeing the best in us — in fact, there are now more of us who are showing the best in us than those of us who are still caught in 'the role of acting out division and separation'. And it is this sharp polarization of experiences today — never before seen in our history — that speaks of a final test in our schooling. The light of the rising Sun of the Sixth Age is enjoining us to let go of the schooling process… that it is time to stop pretending we are separated from each other, divided into factitious roles… that it is time to re-focus on our essential nature as Love and Compassion, wisely applied… that it is time to let go of the need for Suffering… that it is time to acknowledge we are journeying together towards 'somewhere' beyond Space and Time — to the farthest Horizon.

As the Morning Star of the Sixth Age rises in the East, so is the recognition of our essential nature growing in us. It will be a quick awakening — it is already happening! No one is going to be left behind! 'The Sphere of Suffering" — our planet — is becoming 'the Sphere of Love and Compassion'. There is no stopping this, because…

When we re-focus on our essence as Love and Compassion, Suffering ends!

And so the Stanza and the stars remind us today of the purpose of our going and of our essential nature as 'the Prodigal Ones'!

★

The Ending of All Nights

Giving IT no respite, the Two pursued the Third wherever IT went — no place was safe from Them or beyond Their reach. They had taken many a face to cloud Its wits and to mirror Its wants. Each one charming IT to be in the image of Themselves. And thus the Third had been at times one of Them, at others its inverse — but never who IT was Itself.

Such a long time the chase had carried on, the Third had no recollection of Its name — although, buried deep in Its heart lay a doorway opening to THAT who was Its real Self.

Unbeknown to the Two, though, the chase was also changing Them — it wasn't in Their nature to acknowledge who They were, Their lives spent on snaring all who came Their way.

And thus for aeons the chase went on, triumph after triumph over the Third the Two claiming to Themselves. Yet, such was the nature of the Third that with Its very presence in Space and Time nothing could remain the same.

And at last, cornered against the wall of Time, tired of the chase and with no strength left, the Third decided to confront the Two. Thus, taking a quick turn, Iᴛ did what Iᴛ hadn't done before — Iᴛ looked at Them face to face!

Lo, all things came to a standstill — for the first time They saw each other in the light of day, and the Three looked all the same! — Who was who, none of the Three knew then!

And with this, for Them, Time and Space ceased to be. No more days, no more nights — the Three were now One… Tʜᴇ Oɴᴇ — ready to start a new Song of Creation unlike the previous ones.

★ ★ ★

Commentary

This peculiar Stanza was left by the Ancient Teachers as *a synthesis* of the teaching They wanted to offer us with the *"Stanzas of The Dawn"*. It contains several layers of symbolism, each requiring for its interpretation a different "altitude" in consciousness.

One layer of symbolism refers to the cosmological relation, and the interaction, of the Two Origins of our Universe (i.e. *'the Impulse to Be'* and *'the Impulse to not-Be'*) with the Third Emanation (i.e. *The Thinker*) — interaction which was already commented in *Stanza X*.

Another layer of symbolism refers to the journey of identity-discovery of Humans along Space and Time — commented in *Stanza IX* when referring to our triune nature as *a 'beast' who becomes an Angel, plus a God, plus The One.*

A third layer of symbolism refers to the process of 'making of the beast an Angel'; in other words, making of the three aspects of our persona a 'one' — i.e. making of our mind, our feelings and our vital activity a one integrated whole that is fully controlled by one's self.

Yet, there is still another and higher layer of symbolism that refers to something more profound in us, and that only a few teachings on the Perennial Wisdom address. Let's comment on this other layer of symbolism, since it provides a synthesis of all the *"Stanzas of The Dawn"*:

The central thread running along all the Stanzas is that we, Humans, are on a journey of identity-discovery — a journey through Space and Time, and a journey for which we have clothed ourselves in, and have surrounded ourselves with Diversity at every turn — all with the purpose of actualizing our essential nature as *Torchbearers of Sacrificial Will and Compassion* and as *Dragons of Wisdom.*

Yet Diversity isn't just in our external experiences. It isn't just about race, gender, cultural background, religious persuasion, economic wellbeing, education, evolutionary development, and so on. This *Stanza XII* reminds us that a more essential Diversity characterizes each of us in our very Self — *a diversity in Identity,* or in simpler terms, *a diversity in our psychological nature.*

We have already reviewed that each of us is *a triune being* who is sourced by an ESSENCE for which we have no conception at this point in our development. We reviewed that we are *a 'beast' who becomes an Angel* (a persona), plus *a God* (a Soul), plus *The One* (a Spirit) — and that these three are sourced by an eternal and infinite SOURCE or ESSENCE, *The One Source of All.*

This *Stanza XII* takes us further in understanding our journey of identity-discovery. It tells us that *the form* we clothe ourselves with at each of those three levels of our being *is not us,* but that those forms belong to Orders of Beings who are our companions on this journey and who give us temporary identities while we learn from and master the psychological characteristics of their natures.

For instance, we all can attest that our physical body has tendencies or instincts which easily take us in certain directions, at times overruling our will and common sense… that our desires and emotions do the same at their level, pulling us here and there into desire and emotional situations which can overwhelm us… and that our minds do the same, many times running without control and flooding us with thoughts that seem to have a life of their own and that don't leave us alone.

This all happens because those three levels of our being aren't us… because they are the natural psychological tendencies of Orders of Beings who provide for us a physical, a desire-feeling and a mental form while we learn to be our Selves… because, in their essence, those Orders of Beings are still identified with psychological tendencies natural to the Two Origins of the Universe.

However, and so the Stanza reminds us, this constitution of our forms is the result of a planned design. Through the forms those Orders of Beings provide to us, we experience *states of identity* and *a psychological diversity* which weren't, at first, in our inner Essence. But we aren't the only ones who are learning in this relationship. Those Orders of Beings are learning from us those levels of *awareness* which are already in us — and with this they develop a capacity to *hear* and *see* the greater Song of Creation of our Earth and Sol System so that They can, at some point, and like us, contribute fully to it.

> The subject of these other Orders of Beings in our multi-dimensional form is vast and beyond this commentary, and there are other works on the Wisdom that deal with it in a certain depth.* Suffice is to say here that those Orders of Beings provide each of us with the opportunity to experience and learn a psychological diversity.

A very important point to emphasize here is that we can always be in control of that learning process — that our Self is "the Third" mentioned in the Stanza. Of course, as the Stanza also reminds us, taking back control of our journey is a process for which the many cycles of incarnations provide us with the opportunities

---

* More on this subject is found in the books by Alice A. Bailey, published by the Lucis Trust Foundation.

to do so. It is truly a process of getting tired of identify-
ing with those identities that aren't ours, and of choos-
ing to face them directly to arrest their power over us
— it is this process that the Stanzas address when referring to 'the beast becoming an Angel'.

But let's not stop here in our interpretation of the symbolism of this *Stanza XII* and dare to face the fact that
also at the Soul and at the Spirt level we are being provided with the experience of other states of identity
and with a psychological diversity, at those levels, by
other Orders of Beings.

For instance, on our journey, at a certain stage — when
'the beast is becoming the Angel' — we are attracted to
and identify with 'being religious' or 'being spiritual',
with aspirations to become a better person, with plans
to make things better for others, with a drive 'to be
good', etc. All these psychological tendencies which
arise in us at some point on our journey, apparently
out of nowhere, are also made possible in us by an Order of Beings Who in themselves are what we call by
the vague name of "Soul" — in our sub-conscious we
actually have the knowledge of this, and in various cultures this Order of Beings is called "Guardian Angels",
or by an analogous term.

Again, the Stanza reminds us that those stages of our
journey during which one assumes 'identities of Soul'
are just that, psychological stages from which we must
distill their essence to incorporate them in our *psychological diversity,* and then leave the stages behind to enter into new ones.

And so after our experience with the 'identities of Soul'

the journey keeps going at much more exalted levels — those levels we call by the vague term 'Spirit' — where we do the same: Assume 'identities of Spirit', distill their essence, incorporate them in our *psychological diversity*, and then leave those stages behind to emerge into a state of Pure Being where there is no need for more of those experiences.

In the Sixth Age that we are now entering, this theme of the journey of identity-discovery, and of the psychological avenues it takes us through, is going to take a central stage in our lives. Our Sciences, our approach to Religion and to Spirituality, our use of Art, our Philosophies and Social Organization, and our forms of decision-making and Government are all going to reflect, and be refined in ways that will foster that journey for all.

All those developments are in our future, near and far. However, the reason *Stanza XII*, and all the other *"Stanzas of The Dawn"*, is given to us in the present moment of transition from one Age to another, is because the transformation of our identity from 'fixed' beings in Time and Space, limited by them — which is how we all currently feel about ourselves — into masters of our journeying has already begun. We are tired of 'the chase' and about to turn around to face those identities that aren't ours.

The *"Stanzas of The Dawn"*, left by the Ancient Teachers and kept alight by all the many Teachers throughout the Ages, thus, illuminate for us the way we are now traveling as Humans on Earth — at this very critical moment. They are telling us that we are on a journey which is about identity-discovery… that this journey is about experiencing Diversity… that Diversity is a learning immersion to actualize our Love nature… that this Diversity isn't just about external factors, but that our very timeless and non-spatial Self is becoming the sum total of the identities of many Orders of Beings. And all of this because we have a destiny, a destiny which the nascent Sixth Age is starting to reveal and clarify for us — and that will do so with increasing clarity as we acknowledge that we are One Humanity and One Planet, and as we act and live in that acknowledgement.

Torchbearers of Sacrificial Will and Compassion, plus *Dragons of Wisdom* — this is who we are… this is what the decades and centuries to come will reveal of us… this is the promise at…

The Dawn of the Age of the Magicians

* * *

The End

About the Author

Both, *L. Z. Dáin* and the works made available under this name were born from the present need to cast a light on the journey we human beings are traveling on this Earth. Our sciences and religions, our studies on history, our philosophies and our art, and our educational systems, regardless of their advances, do little to illuminate the path through Time and Space that we started traveling in a distant past and that will take us to a distant future. We human beings have arrived at a moment in our history when we are ready to face that journey and add the weight of our will power, of our creative capacities and of our love to make it joyful, easier, more productive, and closer to the intended goal — instead of all the pain, suffering, and trial and error we have endured until now.

Most of the works penned by *L. Z. Dáin*, though not all, are in the form of storytelling in the genre of Science Fiction — more specifically, in the sub-genre of *Visionary Science Fiction*. There is a reason for this choice:

> Storytelling bridges in us the sub-conscious with the supra-conscious, and in so doing it 'speaks' to the innermost self in each of us, eliciting realization and understanding at the conscious level.

Visionary Science Fiction was chosen because in Science Fiction, even though this genre pushes the present-day boundaries of our understanding and of our sciences towards greater horizons, most times the imagined future of scientific and technological advances, and of social and environmental changes, is nothing more than a transplant into that imagined future of our present psychological and social situation on Earth, and of the challenges we face today. Visionary Science Fiction seeks to avoid that. In storytelling of this nature, not just the scientific and technological advances are pushed to greater and positive horizons, but the natural world and human beings themselves — their psychology, their understanding of themselves, and their development and lives — are also envisioned in greater heights than those achieved so far.

The central principle in Visionary Science Fiction is:

> *The Universe in its entirety, and we all with it, is advancing or evolving along a path of an ever-growing perfection, and the future cannot be less than the present but better, brighter and more.*

*

The name *L. Z. Dáin* is a pen name chosen to express the guiding principle in the works of storytelling that constitute the story universe so created — *Tales of the Horizon Story Universe* — and in other works of visionary philosophy.

The letters *L* and *Z* were selected from the expression "Limitless HoriZon" so that the two would sound harmoniously with each other.

The word *dáin* is a grammatical form of the word *dán*, which is an Old Gaelic term with various meanings that have evolved through time. It is usually translated as *bard*.

Thus, the loose expression that inspired the name *L. Z. Dáin* is:

Storyteller of Greater Horizons!

* * *

Writings by L. Z. Dáin

Visionary Science Fiction

Tales of The Horizon™

www.talesofthehorizon.com

★

Visionary Philosophy

Dawn of the Age of the Magicians

www.dawnofthemagicians.com

★

Fireside Stories & Letters

www.lzdain.com